# A BOSS AND A HOOD CHICK

## MZ. BIGGS

Cole Hart
SIGNATURE NOVELS

**A Boss And A Hood Chick**

Copyright © 2021 by Mz. Biggs

All rights reserved.

Published in the United States of America.

This is a work of fiction. Names, characters, places, and incidents either are the products of the author's imagination or are used fictitiously. Any resemblance of actual persons, living or dead, businesses, companies, events, or locales is entirely coincidental. The publisher does not have any control and does not assume any responsibility for author or third-party websites or their content.

Published by Cole Hart Signature, LLC.

**Mailing List**

**To stay up to date on new releases, plus get information on contests, sneak peeks, and more,**

*Go To The Website Below...*

**www.colehartsignature.com**

## CHECK OUT THESE OTHER GREAT BOOKS BY MZ. BIGGS:

See What Had Happened Was: A Contemporary Love Story (Part: 1-3)

Yearning For The Taste of A Bad Boy (Part: 1-3)

Dirty South: A Dope Boy Love Story (Part: 1)

Falling for A Dope Boy (Part: 1-3)

Feenin' For That Thug Lovin' (Part: 1-3)

A Bossed Up Valentine's (Anthology)

Jaxson and Giah: An Undeniable Love (Part: 1-2)

Finding My Rib: A Complicated Love Story (Part: 1)

In love With My Cuddy Buddy (Part: 1-2/Collaboration)

Your Husband's Cheating On Us (Part: 1-3)

From Cuddy Buddy To Wifey: Levi and Raven's Story
(Standalone/Collaboration)

In Love With My Father's Boyfriend (Standalone)

Your Husband's Calling Me Wifey (Standalone)

She's Not Just A Snack... She's A Whole Buffet: BBWs Do It Better
(Standalone)

Blood Over Loyalty: A Brother's Betrayal (Standalone)

Married to the Community D (Part: 1-2)

Downgraded: From Wifey to Mistress (Part: 1-3)

A Mother's Prayer (Part: 1-2)

Heart of A Champion... Mind Of A Killer (Standalone)

Turned Out By My Husband's Best Man (Standalone)

Ain't No Lovin' Like Gulf Coast Lovin' On The 4th of July (A Novella)

This Is Why I Love You (A Novella)

The Hood Was My Claim To Fame (A Novella)

A Killer Valentine's (Anthology)

Bouncing Back After Zaddy Gave Me The Clap (Standalone)

Tantalizing Temptations in New Orleans (An Erotic Novella)

Santa Blessed Me With a Jacktown Boss (Novella)

Diamonds and Pearls (Standalone)

Dating A Female Goon (Standalone/Collaboration)

Pregnant By My Best Friend's Husband (Part: 1-2)

Wifed Up By A Down South Boss (Thug Love Collection)

Creepin' With The Plug Next Door (Part: 1-3)

Creepin' With My Co-Worker (Part 1)

Crushin' On A Dope Boy: Cashae and Tay (Box Set)

The Autobiography of A Boss's Wife (Collaboration)

Scorned By The Love Of A Thug

The Thug Is Mine (Part:1/Collaboration)

Every Dope Boy Got A Side Chick: Kenyon & Milani's Story (Box Set)

## AUTHOR'S NOTE:

Please take the time to leave an honest review on either Amazon or Goodreads after reading the book. Your support is greatly appreciated. Also, feel free to reach out to me anytime via the contact information listed below. Happy Reading... ☺

-Mz. Biggs

***Want to connect with me? Here's how:***

Email: authoress.mz.biggs@gmail.com
Twitter: @mz_biggs
Instagram: mz.biggs
Goodreads: Mz. Biggs
Facebook: Authoress Mz. Biggs
Look for my Reading Group on Facebook:
Lounging with Mz. Biggs

## ❧ I ❧

## NAKOSHA (KOKO)

"*H*er friends and mom hate me *(go)*
   *Lay down on the bed, do the crybaby (mmm)*
*She ain't gave me none of that pussy in a while*
*She had the boy waitin', I don't mind waitin' (come here)*
*Oh, you ain't gon' respond to my texts? (Oh, yeah?)*
*Want me keep on my diamonds, we sex? (What's your name?)*"

As *Cry Baby* by Megan Thee Stallion ft. DaBaby played, I
seductively worked my body around the tall gold-coated pole
that was strategically placed in the center of the club. I made
sure to climb all the way to the top of it and slowly yet gently
slide back down it, while rolling my hips and popping my pussy,
hitting the floor in a full split. That shit always drove the patrons
in the club crazy. I was the last dance of the night, which could
be both a blessing and a curse. The blessing was that I was the
best dancer in this bitch, and niggas was flocking to see my ass
do something strange for a piece of change. The curse was that
the niggas had to wait all night for my ass to hit the stage, and
the other bitches could've weaseled all of their money away from
them before I touched down.

*Two more months of this shit,* I thought to myself as a few men
came and sprinkled some ones over my ass. I wanted to roll my

eyes and go off on them because I felt like I danced my ass off and they should've been thrown some damn twenties, fifties, and hundreds. People thought being a stripper was easy, but that shit required just as much work as going to a nine to five. Hell, if you asked me, strippers did more and had more to lose than people who worked regular jobs. We had to keep our bodies right and have the mental capacity to deal with random ass folks putting their hands all over us. The shit could be annoying as fuck, but it paid the bills.

"Aye, get the fuck out the way. You see I'm trying to get to that pussy," I heard a man yell out of nowhere. It was evident that he was drunk. I kept moving my body and began to survey the room. My nerves were getting the best of me, and I was debating over whether I needed to get off the stage or not. Security ran over to the guy to see what the commotion was while I made contact with the sweeper. I wanted him to go ahead and start picking my fuckin' money up because if a fight broke out, I wasn't about to be running and leaving my shit behind. Bitches so grimy they'd come pick your money up off the floor, knowing it's not theirs, yet they'd keep it like it was.

Darrell followed my cue and began sweeping up the money around the floor as my song came to an end. When it was over, I studied the room more as people stood up and hollered and clapped for me. They were asking for an encore, which I had no problem doing, but not tonight. I had a big test that I needed to get home to study for, and I needed to make sure my son was good. Besides, we were supposed to be celebrating his birthday that weekend, so I needed to get as much rest as I could.

"You got it?" I asked Darrell, who'd made his way up to the stage to start collecting that money as well.

"Yeah. Go ahead and change and I'll meet you in the locker room," he advised me. He didn't have to tell me twice. I rushed to hop off the stage.

Leaving the stage, I decided to go over to the bar and grab a drink before going to the locker room. *What I do that dumb shit for?* I was stopped every five seconds by niggas and bitches asking for a lap dance, my number, and some even offered to take me home. They had me fucked up. I was a stripper, not a prostitute. I wished people would get that out of their heads. Just because a bitch had a banging ass body and took her clothes off to survive, didn't mean that she sold pussy in the process. Bitch, I was a mother. I did have some respect for myself.

In fact, the only reason I started to strip was because of my son. I'd gotten pregnant when I was sixteen, but I didn't have my baby until I was seventeen, and my parents put me out. My father was a pastor, and my mother was a social worker. They were some of the biggest hypocrites I'd ever met, but they stayed playing holier than thou. Getting pregnant was the worst mistake I ever could've made. I was suddenly a disgrace to them. I was even told not to step foot back inside of their church. Now, what kind of a pastor was always quick to talk about forgiving people and not passing judgment, but his ass constantly did it? A lot of them. My father was the worst one of them all. After all of the affairs he'd had, all the money he'd stole from the church, and the outside child he had, you would've thought that he would've been the first person to have my back, but nope. He was the first one to call me a slut and tell me that I was no longer a part of the family. Yep, the damn pastor. It was all good though. My grandmother allowed me to move in with her. She didn't have much, but she loved me and let me know that I was welcomed to anything that she had.

By the time I was about to graduate high school, my grandmother had gotten sick. Even though I got pregnant and chose to keep my baby, I still managed to graduate high school. So for the people that say it wasn't possible, ISSA LIE! Anything was possible if you wanted it bad enough. Anyway, I went from walking off the stage at graduation to bouncing my ass on the stage at Blue Royalty. It was one of the most poppin' strip clubs in Jackson. Fantasy was my stage name. I chose that name because my boyfriend, Nate, always told me that a woman like

3

me was part of every man's fantasy. I was still trying to figure out what exactly he meant by that.

One thing people failed to realize about me was that I was a dreamer, and when I dreamed of anything, I was determined to obtain it. I attended Mississippi College and was working toward two degrees. Yeah, your girl had a double major. My first major was communications with a concentration in journalism, and my second major was in business accounting. I only had two years left. Stripping not only paid my bills, but it also helped me to pay for school so I wouldn't have student loans. It was hard as hell, but like I said, I was determined to make sure I reached my goals.

"You did great, boo," the bartender, Pepper, told me before giving me a hug. "The usual?" she asked.

"Thank you and yes, girl. I'm so glad the night is over. I'm taking the next few days off," I announced.

"Really? Why you taking off?" she inquired.

"It's my son's birthday weekend, and I want to take him out of town. He needs to have a little fun. Plus, I have a big test coming up next week. I'll be able to have fun with my son and study in peace," I happily informed her.

"I know that's right, girl. Anything for our kids. Tell lil' man I said happy birthday and good luck on that test, girl," she cooed and handed me a glass of Crown Apple and Coke.

Turning the glass up, I gulped it down like a pro. My nerves were on a thousand because I could only imagine the bullshit I was going to have to go home to. Shaking my nerves off, I headed to the locker room to change so I could go home. There was always some mess going on at home. Prayerfully, Nate wouldn't be on the bullshit tonight knowing that we had a busy weekend planned. Considering how he was, that was wishful thinking. He didn't give a damn what was going on. He always had to make something about him. I sighed as I slammed my locker shut.

"You ready?" Kita, my best friend, asked.

"Yeah. Let's do this," I replied as we walked out of the club.

We bid our farewells as she hopped in her 2018 Toyota Camry, and I got inside of my 2017 Honda Accord. You'd think we'd be driving something better considering we were the two baddest bitches in the club and made the most money, but we were conservative; at least I was. We had bigger goals, and splurging wasn't going to help us obtain them. I could admit that Kita did spend more money than me, but she had that option. She didn't have a man or a child, so she could live her best life.

My whole ride home was done in complete silence. I even rode with my driver's side window down to allow some of the fresh air to help me clear my head and prepare myself for whatever argument Nate was going to want to have tonight. Reaching the apartment complex, I parked my car and sat there for a while. Letting out a deep sigh, I prepared myself for what was to come as I exited the car and headed inside.

# NATE

C hecking the clock on my phone for what seemed like the hundredth time, I immediately became agitated with KoKo. She was supposed to have been home by now. My mother always told me she was a hoe, but I kept trying to give her the benefit of the doubt. *Just can't trust these stripper hoes*, I thought to myself.

My eyes scanned the room that we shared. It wasn't the best, but it wasn't the worst either. Being a man that was once home-less made me thankful for anything that I could get my hands on. Most of the furniture was old because we got it when we moved out of her grandmother's house. I kept telling her that we needed to upgrade things, but since she was so determined to finish school before wasting money on big things, we had to settle for what we could get.

Nakosha was the first woman I ever really loved. She showed me more love than my own mother did. I met her when she was only sixteen years old. She was walking down the street with some other little fast ass neighborhood girls, and I was a simple corner boy. Being that I was twenty at the time, you would've thought that I had my shit together, but I didn't. Like I said, I was still a simple corner boy.

Being raised by a single mother and watching her struggle, when I got old enough to hit the streets and try to take care of her, I did. I started slanging when I was only seventeen. The one thing I told myself about selling drugs was that it was something I was only going to do temporarily. My dream was to become a rapper. Nobody couldn't tell me that I wasn't fye as hell when it came to getting on the mic. The money that I made from the streets went toward making sure the bills were paid at home. Anything I had left went toward my studio time.

It was hard to believe that I ended up homeless when I was making some money on the streets. Truth be told, that was all on my mother. See, when it came to paying the bills in the house, I always gave the money to my mother and allowed her to handle things. At least I thought she was handling things. It turned out she was paying bills here and there. One particular month, she came to me and told me that we were about to be evicted because we were three months behind on the rent. I spazzed out on her ass because she mismanaged the money that I busted my ass to get. She told me to leave, and I did without ever looking back.

The reason I was homeless at that time was because I'd used all the money that I had left to pay for my studio time. I figured that if I stayed in there, making some bangin' ass music, I'd be able to fast forward my dream of making it big. That was until I laid eyes on KoKo. She was beautiful, no doubt about it. She was young, but the way her hips seductively swayed, the way she suggestively licked her lips, and the twinkle in her eyes when I looked at her showed me that she was more than ready for what I was putting down. It helped that she was hood and ratchet as fuck too.

"Baby?" KoKo called out to me as she pranced inside the apartment. That quickly removed me from my thoughts, and I was ready to go to war. There was no reason for her to be coming in the house as late as she was.

"Where have you been?" I quizzed.

"At work. Where do you think I've been?" she returned.

"Don't answer my question with a question," I yelled. "You should've been home by now," I continued.

"I went on late. Why are you questioning me like that?" she probed, rolling her eyes at me. Nothing infuriated me more than a bitch with a fucked-up attitude. There I was, worried about her ass, and she wanted to get smart with me. She was the one in the wrong, coming in the house all late and shit like she didn't do nothing.

"Because I don't believe you. It seems like each night, you come home later and later," I fussed, grabbing her by the wrist.

"Let go of me. What the fuck are you doing?" She jerked away from me and fell forward. KoKo face-planted on the floor hard as hell. She stayed there for a while which scared me. I thought she bumped her head and knocked herself out.

Frantically, I squatted down next to her and turned her over to check to make sure she was still breathing. There was no way I'd be able to explain what happened to anybody, especially our son. He'd never forgive me if she died and I was the cause of it.

**Smack... Smack...**

Smacking KoKo in the face, I was desperate to get her to wake up. When she wouldn't move, I ran inside the bathroom. We always kept this yellow plastic cup in there for water. It was something her grandmother always did, and she carried it on when we got a place of our own. I grabbed the cup and filled it with water before running back inside the room with KoKo.

**Whoosh...**

After splashing the water down on her, she still didn't move. The only choice I had was to call 9-1-1. Searching in my Levi's jeans, I pulled my phone out and proceeded to call when out of nowhere...

**Cough... Cough...**

KoKo started coughing and coming to. My heart rate started to slow as I began working on controlling my breathing.

"Baby? Baby? Are you okay?" I began to play the role of a

concerned boyfriend. In all actuality, I was more concerned about what would've happened to me if she would've died than I was about something actually happening to her.

"Wh-h-h-hat happened?" she groggily asked.

Thankful that she'd forgotten what happened, I simply stated, "You fell." If she didn't remember what happened, why would I be a fool and tell her? I'd be setting myself up for her to try to leave me, and I didn't have time for that. She was my cash cow. There was no way I was going to tell her what happened, so she could try to dip out on me.

When our son was born, I opted to give up the street life for our family. It wasn't like I was making much out there anyway. Depending on KoKo was what I'd grown accustomed to, so I really had nowhere else to go. Plus, not only was she footing the bills at home, she was also financing my studio time. I couldn't allow her to walk away from me over a simple mistake.

Helping KoKo up off the floor, I took her straight to the bedroom and helped her get into the bed. With any luck, she'd fall asleep and wake up in the morning not remembering any of this.

## 3

# NAKOSHA (KOKO)

The weekend flew by, but we had a blast. I couldn't remember the last time I'd been able to relax the way that I did. Nate and I didn't get into any arguments, which was great. We were able to celebrate our son, and I was able to get some studying done.

"You ready for your test?" Nate asked me as I sat on the edge of our full-sized bed, reviewing the study material for my test one last time.

"I really don't have a choice at this point. The test is today."

"I think you'll do good. You working tonight?"

"Yeah, I need to go in to make up for the time I missed out on over the weekend. I'll try not to stay gone too long," I told him.

"Stay as long as you need to. I trust you. Matter of fact, why don't you go home with Kita and make a girls' night out of it," he suggested.

"Huh? Are you drunk?" I quizzed. He had to be out of his mind for even thinking I would stay out with my friend and not be home to see my son wake up in the morning. His ass was up to something.

"Why I got to be drunk? You just do so much for me and the

baby. It's time that you do something for yourself. When was the last time you went out with your best friend or any of your friends?"

"I see her every day. I don't need to go out with her. I'm a mother, and my motherly duties come first. Besides, I go to school and I have a man at home. I can't be doing all that stuff single women do."

"Single women? Baby, staying over at your friend's house does not mean you are single."

"Drop the subject, Nate. I don't know what's running through your mind, but I'm not staying over at anybody's house. This is where I pay rent, and this is where I'm going to lay my head. Now, I'm going to finish getting ready so I can go to class. I don't want to talk about this again," I told him and left out the room. Walking away was the best thing for me because if he said the wrong thing, it would have me all messed up in the head, and I couldn't have that.

Hopping in the shower, I quickly cleaned myself as I recalled everything that I'd been studying in my head. It was my final exam for my multimedia journalism course. That was one of the final courses I had to take for my bachelor's degree. Truth be told, I've been going to school during both the fall and spring semesters and even taking classes during both summer sessions. That was because I wanted to make sure I had all of the hours I'd need to graduate with both of my degrees within four years.

"Can we talk?" Nate entered the bathroom and asked.

"Can we not do this right now? I really have to get to class. I don't want my mind all over the place when I go take my test," I truthfully commented to him.

"Come straight home after your test so we can talk. I don't want you thinking the wrong thing of me," he chided.

"Okay," I said, even though I really didn't want to talk to him about whatever the hell he had going on. I was sure it would only lead to another fight.

Exiting the bathroom, I searched the room for something I

could throw on. It didn't have to be fancy. In fact, I wanted it to be comfortable since I'd be sitting for a while to complete my test. I grabbed my Cocoa Butter lotion off the dresser and went over to the bed. Propping my left leg up on the foot of the bed, I squirted some lotion on my leg and proceeded to rub it in.

"You sexy as fuck, baby," Nate complimented me.

"Thanks baby," I cooed. I'd take a compliment over an argument any day of the week.

"Let me help you," he insisted.

"I got i-" My statement was interrupted. "Mmmm..." I moaned as I looked down. Nate had crawled between my legs and wrapped his entire mouth around my pussy.

The sound of him slurping and sucking on my pussy filled the room. If Nate couldn't do shit else, he could eat the hell out of some pussy. He feasted on my clit as if he hadn't eaten in days.

"Don't stop, baby," I told him, even though I knew I was running late.

Nate used his tongue to dip in and out of my pussy while using his thumb to rub on my clit. My legs became weak. I thought I was about to fall over. Nate must've sensed it too because he laid down on the floor and pulled me down on his face. I already knew what he wanted me to do. I rode his face like I was riding his dick. He grabbed ahold of my waist and moved my body at the pace he wanted me to move as I grinded my pussy all over his face. It wasn't long before I felt my climax building up.

"I'm about to cum, baby," I announced.

"You know what I want you to do," he lifted me up enough to say. I shook my head even though I knew he couldn't see me.

Picking up the pace, I pushed down and grinded faster on Nate's face. A few seconds later, I lifted my body up and squirted my juices all over him. I glanced down and watched as he held his mouth open with his tongue out to receive as much of my juices as he could. When I was done, he yanked me back down on his face and started slurping on my pussy all over again. It was sensitive as hell from what Nate had just done to me, so I couldn't take anymore. It took everything in me to fight him off.

"What you doing, baby?" he asked, knowing damn well he knew what was up. I simply glanced back at him and noticed him smirking.

"Not funny..." I commented and marched towards the bathroom.

"Damn, I can't even eat yo' pussy without it being a problem," he muttered, stepping inside the bathroom behind me. "You must be fuckin' with another nigga or something. You ain't been giving me the pussy on the regular and you complain whenever I do touch it. What's the problem?"

"Are you seriously doing this right now?"

"Hell yeah. Who the fuck is he?"

The reason I went into the bathroom was to clean myself up but fuck that. I'd rather risk smelling like fish than to allow him to knock me off my A-game and I end up failing a major test. Pushing past him, I left the bathroom and reentered the bedroom. Tossing on a pair of black tights, and a T-shirt, I slid my feet inside of my Tommy Hilfiger flip-flops. Putting my hair up in a messy ponytail, I grabbed my keys, backpack, and purse and headed toward the front door. I made sure to stop at my son's room to love on him before I finally left.

"Well bye to your mufuckin' ass too," I heard Nate say. I threw my hand in the air as if I were telling him bye and kept walking.

Inside the car, I opened my Pandora app and put it on my R&B station. I allowed the station to play the whole time I drove. That was so I'd be able to calm my nerves. As I neared the campus, I once again ran through everything I could remember from what I'd been studying for the test.

*Beeeeppppppppp...*

Glancing down for a second, I quickly looked up when I heard someone laying on their horn. I glimpsed over to see who it was only to lock eyes with one of the sexiest men I'd ever seen.

"Watch where you're going!" he hollered out the window. Flicking him off, I drove on until I found a parking spot near the building I had to test in.

Throwing my car in park, I hopped out and ran toward the classroom. I wasn't sure how this was going to play out, but I was five minutes late and the class had already started. Professor Dinkins shot me a look of disgust as I entered the room. She hated when anybody arrived to class late; especially when it was me.

"Tardiness is not acceptable, even on the last day of class," she told me.

"I understand and I'm sorry. I was almost involved in an accident," I tried to explain even though that wasn't the complete truth.

"Almost doesn't count. That will be a deduction from your test grade."

"A deduction? Why when you haven't even passed the test out?" I was furious. I always thought she was picking on me, and today confirmed the shit.

"Argue with me and you won't get to take the test at all," she commented. That was the only reason I shut my mouth. In my head, I made a mental note to cuss her ass out as soon as I walked the stage and got my degree.

Taking my seat, I said a silent prayer as Professor Dinkins handed out the exams. She gave me mine last. *She's such a bitch,* I thought to myself as I watched her smirk at me when she handed me the test. Reviewing it, I could've passed out because most of the things on the test were not on the study guide she'd given us. However, I was glad that I went beyond just reviewing the study guide and read through the entire book and other notes that I had.

Roughly forty-five minutes later, I was walking out of the classroom, exhausted. When I got to my car, I sat in there trying to collect my thoughts before finally cranking up and heading home. I could only hope that I'd be able to spend a little time with my son and get some rest before having to go in to work tonight without getting into it with Nate again.

۞

As usual, I was the last person to hit the stage. While thankful for the little sleep I was able to get earlier, I still wished I could've gotten more. Too tired to really care about being at work, I did three table dances and then waited around for them to call me out for my last dance of the night. It wasn't my best night, but I really didn't care. Like I said, I was too tired to really care about being there.

Leaving the stage, I had Darrell start scooping my money and told him I'd meet him in the locker room before I headed back to the bar. Pepper already knew what was up. She could see the look of agitation on my face, so instead of sparking a conversation with me, she handed me my usual. Gulping it down, I thanked her before slamming the glass down on the bar. I was about to head back to the locker room until I laid eyes on the same sexy ass man I'd seen earlier on campus. He marched inside the club commanding respect.

The club was about to close, so I didn't understand how he was even able to get in. The way he dressed and looked screamed boss, so that let me know his ass had some type of pull. Wanting to know more about him, I detoured from my original route to the locker room and went toward him. My plan was to not get too close but close enough to see if I could find out who he was.

"Aht aht, bitch," Pepper stopped me. "You have a whole nigga at home. Why you going that way?"

"Girl, I have a second child at home. I need a nigga. Maybe one like him," I joked, pointing at the unknown man.

"He's dangerous, sis. Avoid him at all costs," she warned me. For some reason, I felt like her ass was trying to cock-block. Since I didn't know for sure what her intentions were and she'd never done anything shady to me before, I took in what she was saying and turned back to take my original route. Not before having her give me another drink. Tonight, might not have been my night, but I was going to find out who the man was one way or another.

"Yasssss, bitch. You did that shit," my bestie, Kita, said as I entered the locker room with my drink in hand. She was fully dressed and ready to go.

"Thanks, sis. Give me a sec and I'll be ready," I told her, taking another sip of my drink and then handing it to her.

Normally, I'd take a shower before leaving to try to get some of the smoke smell off me, but I was too tired tonight. All I wanted to do was go home, soak in the tub, and snuggle up under my son. Quickly, I put on a jogging suit and my UGG boots and was ready to go. Darrell came in with my money. I rushed to count it out and paid the house, and we were on our way out the door.

"Yo, hol' up," a male's voice said. Kita and I both looked around to see what was going on, but we never stopped walking. Too much shit happened in Jackson for us to stop to see who the hell the man was talking to.

"Keep walking, bitch. You got your piece in your purse?" Kita probed.

"Locked and loaded," I replied.

"I said hol' up," the man repeated. Kita's purse dropped as she pulled her gun out and aimed it in the direction of the voice.

"Yo, chill out, ma. I'm just trying to talk to y'all," the man stated, throwing his hands up. Suddenly, laughter could be heard. I searched the parking lot to see where it was coming from. That was when I locked eyes with the mysterious man that I'd saw earlier. He hit me with a head nod, causing me to shyly wave at him.

"Put your hand down, bitch. You don't know what these niggas want," Kita scolded. She was right. Quickly, my hand landed at my side as I continued toward the car.

"I'm not telling you to stop again," the man's voice became louder. A cold chill shot up my spine.

"Bitch, stop movin'. You heard the man," Kita's scary ass rattled off. I shot her a look so cold you would've thought I was shooting daggers at her with my eyes. Both of us stood still as the man approached us. Kita still kept her gun pointed at him. I slithered my hand back inside of my purse so I could locate my gun as well. If something happened, we both were going to be ready.

"What's your name, shawty?" the man asked Kita once he'd gotten up on us.

"Who wants to know?" Kita seductively asked. I shot her another look. How the hell this bitch go from being hardcore as fuck one minute and now she was ready to take her pussy off and hand it to the nigga. I couldn't lie, the nigga was fine as fuck. But he wasn't as fine as the nigga I was eyeing though.

"My name Major. I saw your ass up there on that pole earlier. How long you been working here?"

"Not long. How long did you watch me today?" Kita lied. She knew damn well her ass had been sliding up and down that pole for a good three years.

"Long enough to know that I want to make you mine," he said. "But first, let me see how well you can spell," he commented.

"What the hell does me being able to spell have to do with anything?" Kita snapped.

"I don't want no woman that I have to buy *Hooked on Phonics* for," he remarked, and they both laughed. I couldn't lie, I laughed a little too because it was funny as fuck. Kita was smart, but she did need a little extra help at times. If his ass had already peeped that out, she was in trouble.

"That shit not funny," Kita stopped laughing and stated. No matter how hard she tried to keep a straight face, she couldn't. "Now, what do you want me to spell with your crazy ass?" she asked.

"Spell *me*," he told her.

"M-E," she quickly replied.

"Wrong," he said. My face scrunched up as I eyeballed him.

"Come again," Kita said. She was just as confused as I was.

"That's not how you spell that," he told her. She and I both looked at him like he was a fuckin' fool. He was talking about how she couldn't spell, but it seemed to me that he needed more help than she did if he didn't know how to spell *me* of all words.

"What do you mean? I might not always be the brightest crayon in the box, but I know damn well that there's only one way to spell *me* and that's M-E," she hollered, placing her hand on her hip and tapping her toe on the concrete.

"You forgot the D," he commented.

"D? There's no D in *me*," Kita quipped.

"Not yet," he boasted and walked up on her. Kita turned away from him trying to hide the fact that she was blushing. He got right up on her and swiped his dick across her ass causing her to jump a bit before a smile spread across her face. He must've been really working with something because Kita was not a woman that could easily be impressed.

"Not yet, huh? Who said that it was ever going to happen?"

"Trust me, ma. There's nothing that I want that I can't get."

"What makes you so sure that you want me?"

"I'm not sure, so it's on you to keep me entertained. You think you can do that?"

"Entertaining is what I do for a living. If you haven't figured that out by now, then you are barking up the wrong tree."

"I'm not your average Joe. It takes a lot to keep me entertained."

"Trust me, I got this," Kita assured him.

Kita and Major stood there talking as if I didn't exist. It had me wondering why he told me to stop if his attention was solely on her.

"I'm 'bout to go, bitch. Call me later," I interrupted her to say.

"A'ight sis. Love you," she said. I threw my hand up and proceeded to walk away.

"Who told you to leave, ma?" This came from a different deep, baritone voice.

"Got damn, can a sister leave this bitch in peace?" I fumed as I turned around and locked eyes with the man of my dreams again. "I-I-I-I'm so-so-so-sorry," I stuttered, wanting to kick myself for snapping on him.

"You good. Here." He handed me a torn piece of paper with a number on it.

"What's this for?" I asked.

"Use it..." he said and turned to walk away from me. I never even got his damn name. What kinda shit was that? "Oh..." He stopped and faced me again. "Look me in my eyes so I'll know you're listening when I say this," he advised me.

"Huh?"

"Tonight was your last night dancing. Tomorrow will be your last night in this bitch period and that's only because you're coming to clean out your locker. Don't make me say it twice," he asserted, never blinking an eye.

"Hol' up. How you think you gonna tell me what the fuck to do? You not my man. I don't even know you. I got bills to pay and shit," I honestly spoke. I was mad as hell at the fact that this nigga was trying to run me but didn't know me from a can of paint.

"You heard what the fuck I said," he roared and then marched away from me.

"Ugghhhh..." I muttered before getting inside of my car. I balled up the piece of paper he'd handed me and stuck it in the middle console of my car. "That nigga got me fucked up," I said to myself as I cranked up and drove away.

## ❧ 4 ❧

# NAKOSHA (KOKO)

F inally making it home, I completed my nightly routine where I sat in the car and gathered my thoughts. It was crazy how fucked up my life was when I'd done everything I could to make things better for my son. There I was out there shaking my ass on a pole while Nate sat in the house pretending to be getting himself together and watching our son. It took me a while to compose myself before I grabbed my bag and headed inside.

Unlocking the door, I tried pushing it open, but it wouldn't budge. It was like something was blocking me from opening it.

***Bam... Bam... Bam...***

I started beating on the door, praying that he'd come open it before it woke up one of my neighbors. After a good three minutes of beating, I pulled my phone out of my bra and tried calling him. The phone went straight to voicemail. I was pissed. Attempting to push the door open once more, I got nothing. It just wouldn't move. Placing my back against the door, I tried to push it open that way, but that didn't work either. Sliding down the door, it was clear I was going to end up sitting out there waiting until his ass finally woke up.

"Who the fuck out here doing all this beating?" one of my neighbors snatched their door open and asked.

"Go the fuck back in the house, Michelle. I don't have time for this shit tonight."

"Tonight? Bitch, it's the wee hours of the morning. You waking up the whole damn complex with that beating."

"No, bitch! Your loud ass mouth is waking up the whole complex. Take your nosy ass back in the house before you catch this fade."

"Catch that fade? Bitch, you know you don't want this smoke. You can't seriously think you can beat my ass."

"I'm so sick of your shit," I announced and stood from where I was sitting. I charged toward Michelle's door, but she slammed it shut in my face. That shit caused me to laugh. How the fuck you talk all that shit and when somebody gets ready to entertain the shit you were talking, you running scared? I couldn't stand hoes like that.

"Stupid trick," I yelled at the door before going back over to my door and beating on it again.

**Bam... Bam... Bam...**

"Open this fuckin' door, Nate. I'm tired and I want to get in my bed. Open this sh—" Before I could finish my statement, the door flew open.

"Why you beating on the door like that?" he asked like he was stupid.

"Are you out of your fuckin' mind? Why the hell am I having to beat on the door where I pay the fuckin' bills at?" I stepped inside the apartment and noticed the refrigerator behind the door. "What the fuck!" I exclaimed. "Why the fuck is the refrigerator behind the door and not in the kitchen?"

"I saw a damn rat, so I moved the refrigerator trying to get to it," he stated. I knew his ass was lying because he couldn't even look me in the eyes. That was always the number one sign to his ass lying. Limited to no eye contact at all. It was sad that his clown ass hadn't figured that out in all these years. I shook my head at how he thought he was going to get over on me.

"Do I look dumb to you? If you needed to move the refrigerator, all you had to do was push it to the side. You pushed the bitch clean across the whole damn apartment. Then you blocked the fuckin' door. What the fuck you hiding, Nate?" I questioned.

"I'm not doing this shit with you. You stay trying to find a reason to argue with me. You need to go clean your pussy and get in the bed so I can get off in it. I'm sick of you working at that mufuckin' club anyway. You giving all those niggas my time. You need to find another job," he had the nerve to say.

"How about you get a job and let me stay at home with our son for a while?" I suggested. He started laughing and walked away. "That's what the fuck I thought."

Nate walked toward our bedroom and I followed him closely down the hall. Stopping at our son's door, I twisted the doorknob and was about to step inside. That was something I normally didn't do until I'd gotten out the shower because I didn't want him to smell the smoke and funk on me from the club. I would normally shower before I left the club or right as I walked in the house.

"What are you doing?" Nate asked me.

"I want to see my son," I told him.

"You don't do that until after you shower, and you know that. Why you trying to switch up now?" he asked.

"Why is it a problem for me to see my son? Hell, I carried him and pushed him out of my pussy. You don't dictate when I can and can't see him," I sassed.

"I'm not doing this with you. Go shower, KoKo," he angrily instructed. He came back toward me and stood between me and the door.

"Move, Nate!" I directed, but he stood still. We stood there for about five minutes before I finally said, "Fine." Throwing my hands up in defeat, I headed back toward the living room. When he moved out of the way, I took off running toward the bedroom door.

Opening the door, I noticed there were a few comforters balled up in one corner of the room. I shook my head at how filthy Nate's ass was. He probably laid down in the room with our son and instead of putting the covers back where he found them, he tossed them over in a corner for me to do. Once I reached our son's bed, I kneeled down next to him. He was the reason I danced the way that I did. My plan wasn't to stay in his room long, but for some reason, I had to see my son.

For the longest, all I did was watch him sleep. From the Black Panther night light in his room, I admired his little features. He looked so peaceful with his chunky little face and beautiful long lashes. I would kill for lashes like his. Tamir was three years old and I would move heaven and earth for him. When I was younger and my parents used to talk to me about unconditional love, I never experienced it until Tamir graced this earth.

"Come on before you wake him up," Nate urged me.

"Why the hell are you so pressed about me being in here with my son? You better not be on no bullshit, Nate," I voiced.

I remained there a few more minutes and when I was ready to stand, I put my hands down on the floor to help balance myself. As soon as I reached down with my right hand, I felt something that didn't feel like carpet. Moving my hand around to make sure I wasn't tripping, I started yanking and pulling. By this time, Nate was standing in the doorway practically begging me to go to our room.

"Turn the light on," I directed him trying to figure out what the hell I was pulling on.

"No. You're not about to wake our son up," he rebutted.

"Turn on the fuckin' light, Nate. Something is under his bed," I informed him.

"Get up, KoKo. Your ass is just tired. Ain't nothing under his bed," he replied.

Growing tired of arguing with him, I yanked on what I felt once again. When it didn't move, I sat on the floor and used both of my hands to pull whatever it was from under the bed.

"Aaaghhhhh!" I heard a woman holler. That was when it dawned on me why the cover was in the room. That nigga was fuckin' on the floor in our son's room.

"Muthafucka!" I shouted. Rage filled my body as I stood from where I was on the floor and attacked Nate. He put his hands up trying to defend himself, but my attack was too much. I was hitting him wherever my hands could connect and there was nothing he could do to stop me.

"Get off me, KoKo," he yelled. Suddenly, I felt something pulling and tugging at my hair. It couldn't have been Nate because both of his hands were on me trying to keep me from hitting him. The bitch had come from under the bed and was calling herself helping him. That further infuriated me.

Reaching behind me, I grabbed ahold of her hair and slung her over me. I wasn't sure where that strength came from, but it was real. That was how I knew I was upset. When you muster up the strength to do some shit you never thought you'd ever be able to do, you know you're about to fuck some shit up.

"Mommy... Mommy..." I heard my son's innocent voice. That was the only reason I stopped. That was no way for him to see me. I didn't want him to remember this night every time he looked at me. With any luck, I could get him to go back to sleep and he'd forget all about it.

"I'm sorry, baby," I spoke as I stopped hitting Nate and grabbed ahold of my son. "Get out," I stated through clenched teeth.

"What? Nothing happened, baby. I'm not leaving," he confidently commented.

"Nate, I'm giving you the chance to leave before I make you leave. Please don't push me to do something that I'll regret. That's why you pushed that refrigerator behind the door. You knew I wouldn't be able to get in and it would give you enough time to wrap up what you were doing with her. The fucked-up part is that I've allowed you to sit on your ass and do nothing while I'm out there shaking my ass and allowing drunk ass people to rub all up on me. How could you hurt me like this?" As I spoke, I thought tears would fall, but they didn't. That was when I knew I was done. I was cool. I was calm. I was collected. I was aware of everything going on. All I wanted was for him to leave. I didn't give a damn what he took with him as long as he got the fuck out of my house.

"I fucked up, ma. I'm sorry. You know I don't have anywhere to go," he pleaded. That was shocking considering he'd hurt me time and time again and I let the shit slide. I guess he thought I was going to keep letting him get away with hurting me. When he was caught the last time, he was warned that I wouldn't stand for it any longer. You would've thought he would've taken me serious and did right by me. Clearly, he didn't. It was too late now. The damage had been done and I was over the entire situation.

"You knew you didn't have anywhere to go when you decided to fuck with her. That's your fault, not mine. Get the fuck outta my shit," I barked.

"Fine, fuck you! I'm taking my son with me," he boasted. He got off the floor and came toward me like I was really about to let him take my son. He didn't even want Tamir, but he knew that as long as my son needed to be taken care of, I was going to fork out money to make sure he was good. I'd rather live a very poor lifestyle with no money or no job than to allow that nigga to walk out the door with my son.

"A'ight. Bet," I spoke. Nate glimpsed back at me as if he'd seen a ghost before going over to where his trick was laid out on the floor. She must've hit her head on the wall when I slung her because she wasn't moving.

"You killed her," Nate announced.

"It was self-defense. She attacked me," I said, shrugging my shoulder. "Get out, Nate!" I calmly spoke.

"No, I'm not going anywhere. This is my house too. You have to take me to court and put me out if you want me to leave."

"Come again?"

"You heard what the fuck I said. You know damn well I don't have anywhere to go, and since I have taken up residency here, you have to take me to court and evict me like any other land-lord would." He smirked.

"Oh, I'm going to take you somewhere, and I promise you it won't be to court."

Remembering I'd left my bag in the living room earlier, I placed my son back in his bed before I moved around Nate and his hoe and went straight for the bag. After digging around inside of it and locating what I was looking for, I headed back to my son's room.

"Come on, KoKo. You don't want to do this," Nate pleaded. He had his hands in the air as if he were being robbed.

"This is the last time I'm going to tell you to get your bitch and get the fuck out of my house. If I have to repeat myself again, you're going out in a body bag."

"You wouldn't dare." He had the nerve to cross his arms over his chest as if he were really daring me to shoot him.

*Pow...*

Letting a shot out in the air, I could see pee running down Nate's leg.

"Next time, I'm going to hit my mark," I warned him.

Nate ran to the room, grabbed something, and ran out the door, leaving his trick behind to fend for herself. I took it upon myself to grab her by the hair and pull her out of the apartment. I left her right in the breezeway, butt booty ass naked. I already knew there was going to be some backlash behind the shit, but I had to protect myself. I was tired of letting mufuckas run over me.

Instantly, I went to my room and gathered as much stuff that I thought I would need for a few weeks and ran it down to my car before going back inside the apartment and doing the same for my son. I even went as far as grabbing all of the food out the refrigerator and cabinets and took it out to the car before I bundled my son up and took him out to the car. Luckily for me, I lived in Jackson. You have a better chance of waiting for God to come save you than the police. They were always slow, so I had all the time I needed to make sure we had everything we were going to need. I crunk up the car and backed out of the parking lot.

It didn't take a rocket scientist to realize that this wasn't going to be the last time I saw Nate's ass. However, I hoped and prayed that he'd be scared enough to stay away from me at least for the next few weeks. That would be more than enough time for me to get my mind together.

***Beeeeppppppppp...***

Consumed with my thoughts, I didn't realize that I was sitting at a green light until I heard someone behind me honking.

"Rude bitch," I yelled at them even though I was in the wrong. "If I had a dump truck, I'd backed up over their ass. I should buy one," I said to myself. That caused me to abruptly hit my brakes and think about the fact that while I was gathering things from the house, I left the duffel bag that contained my money from the night. I threw the car in drive and turned around at the next street to head back to my apartment.

When I made it back, I left the car running and hauled ass to the apartment. The door was wide open, so I knew that Nate's ass had been back there. Stepping inside the living room where I remembered last seeing the duffel bag, I was pissed to see that it was gone. I checked every other room to make sure I didn't move it and couldn't remember that I did. It was nowhere to be found. My money was gone. Once again, I'd allowed Nate to make a fool out of me. He was going to have to pay for this shit. He was about to learn that stealing from me was the worst decision he could've ever made.

## 5

# NAKITA (KITA)

**R***ing... Ring... Ring...*
My phone ringing caused me to stir out of my sleep.
Rolling over, I turned on the lamp and blinked a few times to
clear my vision. When I saw the time, I was mad as hell that
someone would be waking me up so early. I barely got enough
sleep as it was, so whenever I did fall asleep, I hated when
people disturbed me. Noticing that it was KoKo calling, I
hurried to answer the phone. Something had to be wrong
because she never called me at this time of the morning.

"Hello. You okay, sis?" I shot up in the bed and began asking
her all kinds of questions.

"No. I'm not okay. I need a place to crash where Nate can't
find me," she exclaimed. Her voice was panicked, and that
worried me even more.

"Where are you? I'm coming to get you," I stated. I
attempted to jump out the bed but was pinned down by the arm
that was wrapped around me.

"Where you going, ma?" he asked.

"My friend needs me," I told him.

"Tell her to call the number," he rebutted.

"What?" I was furious that he was downplaying the fact that

28

my best friend needed me. One thing I was, was a good friend. I didn't give a damn what was going on. I'd drop everything I was doing to get to my friend if she needed me. That was because I knew she'd do the same for me.

Major and I stood in the parking lot talking for a long while after KoKo had left. It started to get cold and I was tired and hungry. We ended up going to IHOP to eat, but even then, neither one of us wanted the night to end so he got us a hotel room. We were staying at The Westin Hotel, which happened to be one of the best hotels in Jackson.

Don't get me wrong, I had thoughts of wanting Major inside of me, but nothing happened. All we did was talk. So damn what? Shit, I was grown. If I wanted to do tricks on his dick, then I could've. The only reason I didn't was because, for the first time, I met a man that was interested in stimulating my mind and not just sliding between my thighs. We sat on the bed and talked about all types of shit. It was refreshing. It made me really curious to know where things could go with us, so I decided it would be best for me to take my time with him. There was no telling where we could end up and I was interested in finding out.

The one thing that touched me the most was him being curious as to why I was stripping. I had to tell him that I didn't have the best life. It wasn't that we were poverty stricken, because that was far from the case. The best way for me to describe my life would be to compare it to New New's life on the movie *ATL*.

My parents were from the hood but when they got older and got a little bit of money, they forgot where they came from. I loved the hood. That was where the realest people and situations happened. Any chance I could break away from my bougie life-style and go back to the hood, I would. They forbade me from hanging in the hood. So, I would sneak off and explore it when-ever possible. I was able to get away with it because even in our bougie neighborhood, I had friends that didn't have expensive cars like me. I would borrow their cars and ride around the hood like I belonged. I'd always have an extra pair of clothes with me so I could dress the part. I even went as far as getting me a thugged out ass boyfriend. He wasn't shit. He cheated on me every chance he could and like an idiot, I would take him back. He was my first real boyfriend. My first love. The first person I gave myself to. I thought we would be together forever, but he fooled me. Like KoKo, I had gotten pregnant when I was in high school. The only difference was that she kept her baby and I didn't. That was a mistake I regretted every time I laid eyes on Tamir.

My parents cut me off when they found out what I was doing instead of understanding my reasoning behind it.

Being a teenager with no money, no dreams, nowhere to go, I did what I had to do. People thought I was hot in the ass because I stayed hanging with the wrong people and on the block, but I didn't even lose my virginity until I got my first real boyfriend, and I was a senior in high school when that happened. Nobody understood that because they'd already formed this stereotypical attitude in regard to me. One thing I would proudly be able to tell my parents whenever we did get back to a point of being cordial with each other was that when I was down and out, none of those bougie people that they wanted me to grow up around helped me out. It was my friends in the hood that made sure I had a roof over my head, food on the table, and clothes on my back. If that wasn't real, I didn't know what the hell real was.

"Kita? Did you hear me?" Major called my name, bringing me back from my thoughts.

"No, I'm sorry. What did you say?" I apologized for not paying attention to him.

"Tell her to call the number," he instructed me.

"Bitch, are you there?" I heard KoKo yelling through the phone.

"Yeah, I'm here," I replied. "Major said call the number," I regrettably told her. I wasn't sure who would be on the other end of the phone when she called the number, and I knew that if I called her for help, she would've come running. That was the reason I regretted telling her to call the number.

"What? Who the fuck is Major?" she quizzed.

"The man from the club," I explained.

"Bitch, I know damn well you ain't give that nigga no pussy," she gasped.

"Damn, you don't have faith in me at all." I snickered a bit.

"Bitch, no, ma'am. We both know how you are, and I'm not calling no damn number for no random ass nigga. Either you coming to help me or you not."

"Damn, bitch, I'm on my way. Send me your location and I'll be there soon." I ended the call and stood up.

"Where you going?" Major sat up in the bed and asked.

"I have to go help her. She has a son. She's not going to take him around no random ass man. She's hood like me, but she doesn't have the freedom to move like I do. If it would've been her by herself, that would've been one thing, but it's not. I have to respect that," I informed him.

"I got you, ma. Let me know when she sends you the location so I can go with you."

As soon as the words left his mouth, my phone went off, notifying me of an incoming text. I knew it was nobody by KoKo sending me her location.

"Let me see the phone," Major spoke. Normally, I would've said hell no because I didn't think anyone should have the right to invade anyone else's privacy, but there was something different about Major. I wasn't about to do anything to make him not trust me or not want to explore the possibility of a relationship with me, so I had no problem handing him my phone.

Unlocking my phone, I tossed it over to him. He scrolled through it for a while and pushed a few buttons before handing the phone back to me. I went through the phone to see what he could've been doing but I didn't see anything.

"What did you do?"

"I sent my boy her location. He'll go get her. Come get back in the bed," he directed.

"No, I'm not doing that. I'm going to help my friend," I fumed. He'd pissed me off just that quick and I was ready to say *fuck you!*

"If you go out that door, it's going to be the worst decision you could've ever made in life," he told me. My head snapped back as I looked at him like he'd lost his damn mind. It showed me that the guy I thought I was going to get to know was just a façade and that he was really an asshole.

Instead of entertaining his last statement, I grabbed everything that belonged to me and exited the room without looking back. KoKo was going to owe me big time for this shit.

When I got inside the car, I opened my texts to where she'd sent me her location. I pushed the location and allowed my GPS to take me to where she was. Coincidentally, she wasn't very far from me. It took me roughly fifteen minutes to get to where she was. Her car was pulled over on the side of the road with the headlights off. It was too early in the morning for this shit. Anything could have happened to her.

"What the hell is going on?" I asked as I jumped out of my car and ran to her.

KoKo sat in her car holding her son in her arms. He was sleeping, and tears were running down her face.

"What happened?"

"Just help me grab my shit, and I'll tell you all about it later. All I want to do is get him in a bed somewhere safe."

"So you just gonna leave your car here? That's not safe," I muttered.

"The police may be looking for me," she blurted out.

"Huh? OMG! Did you kill him?" I questioned right before I gasped and my hands flew over my mouth.

"No, bitch. I should have though," she announced. My eyes grew big as hell. I was worried. What the fuck was she not

32

telling me? I loved her, but I didn't want to be caught up in no bullshit. She owed me the truth. "None of this is going to lead to you going to jail. All I need is for you to get me away from here."

"Where do you want me to take you? We can't go to my place if the police are looking for you, because if someone gives my name as your friend, which they will, they will come straight to my house. You can't go to your grandmother's, because they will go there too."

"Take me to a hotel, and we will figure it out," she mumbled.

"I was just at the hotel. If that was all you wanted, you should've said that on the phone, and I could've gotten you a room. You done made me get mad and leave my nigga only for you to want to go to a hotel. What kind of shit is that?" My hands went to my hips as I began pacing back and forth. Don't get me wrong, I loved my girl, but she did some looney shit sometimes. Now, I could've messed up something good when it could've possibly been an easy fix.

Out of nowhere, four sets of headlights came zoning in on us. My scary ass opened the door to the backseat of her car and dived inside.

"Drive bitch!" I ordered. I was scared as hell. It had me really questioning if coming to help her was the right decision. What had she gotten me into?

"Hold my son," she told me, passing Tamir back to me. She cranked the car and was trying to drive off but we were blocked in.

"What the fuck! Ram their shit and make them move," I fussed.

"Bitch, are you crazy? I can't do that with my son in this car," she fumed, reminding me about Tamir being with us.

"Fuck! What is going on? What did you do? Who is trying to kill us?" I started asking all kinds of questions.

"It's not like that," she tried to explain.

"Like what? Something is going on. You may not have time to explain now, but you need to drive this bitch, hoe!"

Suddenly, another car came flying in and came to a screeching halt. We were both terrified. I kept wondering what the fuck was going on and what KoKo had gotten me into.

"Get the fuck out of the car, Kita," Major's voice boomed in my ear. When I made eye contact with him, I felt myself melting into the seat. The serious look in his eyes had me nervous as hell. I wasn't a fool though. I slid my ass right out of the car. "Go get in my car," he ordered.

"Wait... What about my car?" I quizzed. We lived in Jackson. There was no way in hell I was going to leave my car on side of the road for somebody to steal or vandalize my shit. It wasn't the best car out here, but it was mine.

"JT, drive her car to your spot. We'll come get it in a few days."

"The fuck we will! I don't know him! He not taking my car anywhere!"

"Keys, ma," Major demanded.

"What?" I acted like I didn't hear him.

"Give me the fuckin' keys, Kita. This the last time I'm saying the shit."

"They are in the car," I pouted. Major did something with his head, and JT ran straight over to my car, hopped in, and peeled out. "Wait, my purse and phone are in there."

"You don't need it," Major stated.

"Why are you doing this?" I asked him.

"When I see something I want, I go after it. Either you are going to make this easy or you're going to make it hard, but the choice is up to you," he advised me.

"What did you mean about if I left earlier, it was going to be the worst decision of my life?" I questioned.

"You'll find out later. I don't tolerate the disobedience. I can already tell right now I'm going to have to tame your lil' ass. Don't worry. It'll be just as much fun for you as it will be for me," he spoke, running his tongue along his teeth and rubbing his hands together like Birdman. My eyes bucked again. *Was this nigga thinking he was about to punish my pussy? Ain't no way.*

"I can't leave my friend," I told him.

"He got her," he said, nodding in the direction of his friend who had just gotten out of the other car and was headed toward KoKo.

Glancing down at KoKo, she had an expression of worry and confusion on her face. I couldn't say that I blamed her. We didn't know these niggas. At least, I'd spent a little time with Major to somewhat get comfortable enough with him. How could they expect us to be cool with someone helping her and we didn't even know their name?

The man approached KoKo's car. We both stared at him and wondered what he was about to do. Major grabbed me by the hand and began trying to pull me away. I planted my feet on the ground and tried to stand still. I couldn't leave without knowing what was going to happen to KoKo. It worried me to walk away from KoKo and her son, but something told me if I didn't go with Major, he'd make sure I regretted it.

"Wait... Let me just see what he's about to d-"

Major picked me up and tossed me over his shoulder. He carried me away from KoKo, kicking and screaming. He placed me in the backseat of his car and shut the door. I tried to get out, but I couldn't. That nigga must've put the damn child lock on. There was no way I could get out. I laid down on the seat and was about to try to kick the window out until he got inside the car.

Major looked at me and said, "You can kick my shit if you want to. You won't kick any damn thing else." The tone in his voice let me know that he meant business.

Changing my mind, I sat up in the seat, pouting, with my arms crossed over my chest. Major shook his head, cranked the car up, and drove off. I peered out the back window as we drove away from KoKo. The only thing left for me to do was pray that my girl was going to be okay.

# 6

## MAJOR

Kita's lil' ass was hardheaded as fuck. Normally, I would stray away from the women I couldn't control. However, that shit never worked for me, and I could never find the queen that I really wanted in my corner. When my boy and I got to the club that night and we saw Kita and KoKo, something told us both that they were different. They were rough around the edges, but they were like diamonds. Shit, we figured all they needed was a lil' polishing and they would be good to go. But damn, they were already acting up. I liked her lil' ass, but I wasn't sure if I was ready for the damn headache. Working the streets was already rough on us. Our women needed to be our peace.

The minute Kita left, I hit my boy Hassan up and let him know what was up. He told me he was on his way, and I told him I was too. Kita had made me mad for not listening to me, but I wasn't ready to count her lil' ass out yet. My mind was so focused on her, I even hit my mother up to talk to her about it.

I was raised by a single mother. I never met my father. He was killed three months before I was born. Thankfully, my mother had a strong support system around her. She did the best she could as a single mother, so I made it a point to start making

36

my own money so I could spoil her. The only problem with that was that my mother was deep into the church. She was Jehovah's Witness, which was how she raised me, but in my line of business, that was a religion I couldn't stick with. That didn't mean I wasn't into church.

Mount Vernon on the Rock Calling Jesus Baptist Church was my church home. I'd been going there ever since I was seventeen. At the age of twenty-four, that hadn't changed a bit. My mother and I did early-morning prayer calls every morning, and I prayed at night and throughout the day. I was at church almost every Sunday unless something popped off. I also paid my pastor to give me private Bible study lessons. Was I living the ideal lifestyle? No. But did that mean I didn't deserve to have a relationship with God too? Absolutely not.

When I called my mother, I told her I needed to do our prayer session earlier because I had something important to do. She asked me what it was, and I told her the situation with Kita. She told me I was doing the right thing by going after her and even prayed over the situation with me. That was when I knew that Kita was potentially the woman created for me. That was the real reason I went after her.

There we were, riding back to the hotel, and I couldn't help but to keep glancing in the rearview mirror at Kita. Ma was fine as fuck. She was short as shit too. She couldn't have been no more than five feet four and roughly a hundred fifty pounds. I was sure most of that was in her ass and breasts because she was very shapely. Not to mention those thick ass thighs that I couldn't wait to slide in between. Baby girl had more thighs than Popeye's, and I wasn't mad at that at all. Her hair flowed straight down her back, but I wasn't sure if it was hers or not yet. Normally, there would be some shedding or lace shown somewhere that would help me to identify if it was fake or not, but whoever did her hair slayed the fuck out of it because it looked good as fuck. She was toned everywhere, which let me know that she worked out, and that was right up my alley. I didn't give a damn what was going on around me. I always made it to the gym. That was the best way for me to relieve stress—other than sex. Her nude-colored skin complexion and round face were beautifully flawless. She had high cheekbones with slanted like Chinese eyes that were like a charcoal-black color. I'd never seen anyone's eyes that dark. I did peep that her eye color changed with her mood, which intrigued me more because it helped me to identify when she was mad, scared, happy, and pissed. Yeah, I noticed all of that about her in the short period of time that I've known her. The charcoal black was the color that showed when she was happy. That was the color I adored and wanted to be sure to see all the time. Right now, her eyes were a greenish color. That meant that she was agitated. I would've cared about her being agitated if I weren't feeling the same way.

"Where are we going?" She broke the silence between us. I never responded. Her little ass was on punishment, so she was going to have to earn conversation out of me again. "I know you hear me talking to you," she quipped, but still, I remained quiet.

We pulled up at the hotel, and I got out the car. Tossing my keys to valet, I moved around to the passenger side of the car and opened the door for her. She was sitting there with her arms still folded over her chest, pouting.

"Get out the car, ma," I instructed her. She looked at me and rolled her eyes. There went that feisty shit that I didn't feel like dealing with. It was too early for this shit, and I had a busy day ahead of me.

"I'm not going to get out of this car until you answer me," she chided.

"What is there to answer? You see where we are," I muttered.

"Don't play with me, Major. You want me to move when you say move, but you can't answer one simple question. You not about to keep punkin' me like I'm some weak bitch," she sassed.

Instead of entertaining her negative energy, I said, "Chrome, park this bitch with her ass in it. Make sure you turn the alarm on. If it goes off, then make sure you call the police and tell them somebody trying to steal my shit."

"I got you, boss," Chrome replied as he hopped inside the car. I shut the door to the passenger's side and proceeded to walk inside the hotel.

The staff at the hotel greeted me as I made my way through the lobby and up to my room. I'd hit them with a serious head nod and kept walking. I was tired, so I didn't have time for any small talk. When I reached the room, I used my key to get inside and made sure to lock all the locks to the door before stepping inside the bathroom. Turning the shower on, I allowed the steam to fill the entire room while I undressed. I stood in front of the mirror and admired the abs on my body. I'd put in a lot of work to get them. Kita was going to be mad as hell when summer came because a nigga wasn't going to know what the fuck a shirt was.

Stepping into the shower, the steaming hot water hit my body causing me to flinch a bit, but I never got out. I loved my water to be superhot because it removed the tension in my body. As much shit that I stayed dealing with on a day-to-day basis, I needed to be as relaxed as possible. I even put my head under the running water to allow it to beat down my face and run down my back. I was enjoying my shower until I heard beating on the door. I already knew who it was, so I wasn't in a hurry to get out. I allowed her to beat on the door for at least five minutes so I could finish getting the soap off my body before I exited the shower and wrapped a towel around me. I opened the door with a smirk on my face.

"Why the fuck you do that?" Kita asked, breathing hard as fuck. She stepped in the room and flopped down on the couch trying to regain control of her breathing.

"Do what?"

"Why'd you tell him to turn the alarm on? When I opened the door, it started going off loud as hell. People were looking at me like I was stealing," she fussed. I shrugged my shoulders and walked away from her. I went right back inside the bathroom so I could brush my teeth. She was still in the living room fussing.

It wasn't until I'd finished brushing my teeth that I dried the rest of my body off before moisturizing it with some lotion and going over to the bed. I removed my towel and climbed in bed naked. I shot Kita a look out the corner of my eye to see if she was looking, and indeed, she was. She was almost salivating out of her mouth. The shit was funny, but I couldn't laugh, or it would give it away that I wanted her ass to lust over me.

"What are you doing?" she probed.

"I'm going to sleep. What does it look like I'm doing?" I answered.

"You're naked," she announced.

"That's how I sleep," I muttered. "Look, ma, if you uncomfortable, sleep on the couch. That's on you. We both grown, hell." Once again, I watched her pout. I shook my head before pulling the cover over me and rolling over.

It wasn't long before I heard the shower running. "You used all of the hot water?" she hollered. All I could do was laugh at her crazy ass. Had she come up when I told her to, then we could've showered together and she would've been able to enjoy the hot water as well, but since she wanted to play games, I was going to have to break her ass every time. *Checkmate*, I thought to myself before closing my eyes.

A little while later, my eyes popped open as I heard movement around me. It was Kita coming out of the bathroom. She had a towel wrapped around her head and her body. I wanted her to remove her towel so I could admire every inch of her. I saw her with her work attire on earlier, but I wanted to see her as naked as the day she was born. I wanted to see what my pussy looked like. Shit, if she let me, I wanted to taste that fat mufucka. I knew it was fat because that bitch was playing peek-a-boo through her pants earlier.

Kita climbed in the bed with the towels still wrapped around her. She laid on the edge of the bed, which I thought was funny.

That showed me she had no self-control. She wasn't trying to get too close to me at all. She knew what was up. A nigga was going to slide right on between those damn thighs and fuck the shit out of her.

"Why you so far over there?" I asked.

"Because I'm mad at you. I don't want you touching me right now," she stated.

"Girl, you think I give a fuck? Because I don't. I don't give a fuck about none of that shit you talking. Now, come over here so I can put my dick on your ass."

"Ugh, no! You ain't sticking shit in my ass."

"You must want me to fuck you in the ass because that was not what I said at all. I'm trying to spoon with your lil' freaky ass," I asserted.

"Oh..." she replied.

Hesitantly, she slid over to the middle of the bed. I wasn't about to keep playing with her little ass, so I wrapped my arm around her and pulled her closer to me. Lifting her towel up, I rolled up under her where my dick was touching her ass. She started rocking from side to side. I knew that meant her pussy was getting wet. I even felt her body tensing up as she squeezed her legs together. The shit was funny as hell. I wanted to laugh, but I didn't want her to realize that I was fuckin' with her.

"Good night, Kita!"

"Yeah," she replied. That rubbed me the wrong way. I popped up in the bed and turned the lamp on. Yanking her over on her back, I got on top of her and stared down into her eyes. "What the fuck!" she exclaimed.

"You're really about to piss me the fuck off."

"What I do?"

"Your attitude not cool, ma! Have I done anything to hurt you?"

"No."

"Did I force you into doing anything that you didn't want to do?"

"Hell yeah. You made someone else drive off in my car with all of my money and cell phone in it. What other choice did I have than to come up here?" she fussed.

"Kita, all you had to do was say you didn't want to be here. Do I look like the type of nigga to have to force a chick into doing anything? Bitches drop their panties for me if I just look at their ass."

"Well, I'm not bitches."

"But you're acting like one," I called myself mumbling.

"What did you just say?" she probed, trying to sit up. I wouldn't allow her to move.

"I said you're acting like one. I'm not scared of you. If I say anything once, trust me when I say that I can say the shit again," I told her.

"Don't ever call me a bitch again," she snapped.

"Did I call you a bitch or did I say that you're acting like one? Those are two completely different things," I informed her. She laid there glaring into my eyes. Her facial expression told me that she was not pleased at all by what I was saying to her. "Look, you need to chill out with all of that hood shit. I understand you've had it tough and you've had to play this hard chick most of your life, but you don't have to do all of that with me."

"Whatever. Get off me," she bellowed, trying to push me away. I grabbed her arms and pinned them both down on the bed, over her head.

"Look, I've been trying to give you the benefit of the doubt, but you're pushing your luck. I don't deal with attitudes. If you mad at me, say that shit so we can work it out. I don't do that going to sleep angry shit because all it does is make that anger carry over to the next day, and I don't deal with that shit. I already have enough shit on my plate. You think I want to be dealing with bitch shit from my girl too? If you want to talk this shit out, then say that. Or, I can let you go, and you can leave. I'm not beggin' no damn body," I barked.

Swiftly, she turned her head away from me. The way she

stared at the wall let me know that she was thinking about what I'd said. She had to see how big of a damn fool she was acting. Placing my hand on the side of her face, I turned it to where she was facing me.

"Look at me when I'm talking to you. Don't ever turn away from me or anyone else. You gain their respect and trust when you can look their ass in the eyes. Even if you're lying, look a mufucka in their eyes. That'll fuck them up every time," I educated her. That was real shit that I felt everyone needed to know.

"I'm sorry," she gazed into my eyes and apologized. She began biting her bottom lip before she lifted her head up, and our lips connected. There was no way I could fight her. The chemistry between us was real. I allowed my tongue to enter her mouth. The passion in our kiss was something I'd never experienced before. Not that I placed my lips on every girl that I came into contact with, but out of the few that I did, that was hands down the best kiss I'd ever had.

My dick grew a mind of its own as it started to rise. Not wanting to offend Kita or make her think I was only out for her pussy, I pulled away from her and rolled over on my back. She quickly climbed on top of me and reached for my dick. She glided down on it, causing me to hiss. Her pussy was wet and tight as fuck. That wasn't what I expected. I was in heaven.

"Sssss..." I hissed again as she slowly moved up and down on my shit. My eyes rolled to the back of my head as I enjoyed the pleasure she was giving me.

Kita slowly bounced up and down on my dick before dropping completely down and grinding on it. My mouth popped open, but no sound came out. I felt paralyzed. While unsure of what she was doing to me, I was loving every minute of it. I placed my arms on her hips and began picking her up and slamming her back down on my dick. She began hollering and moaning out loud. I smiled because it was helping me regain control of the situation.

"Slow down," she mumbled, but I wasn't trying to hear that shit. She wasn't thinking about slowing down when she was tightening her pussy muscles around my dick, trying to milk me for every drop of nut inside of a nigga.

Flipping her over and positioning her on all fours, I rushed to put my dick back inside of her like I was fighting to maintain oxygen. Just that quick, I'd grown accustomed to being inside of her. It was the best feeling in the world for me right now. It was actually more enjoyable than counting my money. I never thought anything would be better than that.

"Take this dick," I stated before popping her on the ass. She bucked a few times but continued to throw her ass back on me. She motorcycled back on my dick like she was riding a dirt bike. I damn near lost it.

"I'm cummin'," she announced. I smiled because that was exactly what I wanted to happen. She had to bust before me, or I'd never hear the end of it.

"Naw. Hold that shit in," I demanded.

"I can't. You're fuckin' me too good," she stated.

"Mmmm hmmm... You better hold that shit in," I repeated, smacking her ass a few more times.

"I can'tttttt... I'm cumminnn'..." she wailed as she began shaking. I pulled out of her and watched as she squirted all over the sheets. When she was done, her body dropped down to the bed. I lifted her back up and inserted myself back inside of her. "I can't take anymore, baby," she told me. She was practically begging me to let her rest. I wasn't trying to hear any of that.

"Fuck all that. You wanted to act hard earlier, so you 'bout to pay for all that shit," I muttered as I delivered long, deep, paralyzing strokes to her. The deeper I went inside of her, the louder she screamed. All of that screaming was only turning me on more and making me go hard in the paint trying to blow her back out.

Kita reached down and started rubbing on her clit. That shit was sexy as fuck to me. I started biting on my bottom lip, trying to think of everything under the sun other than busting. She was feeling so good, I didn't want this feeling to end. Then she started squeezing her muscles even tighter around my dick, and I almost lost my mind. I couldn't hold it in any longer.

"Damn, girl. You 'bout to make a nigga bust," I told her.

"Give it to me, baby," she replied. Next thing I knew, she pulled forward, turned where her head would be facing me, and quickly stuck my dick in her mouth. She started sucking my dick as if her life depended on it.

"Shiittttt..." I grunted as I unloaded all of my seeds down her throat. I watched as she sat back and gargled it in her mouth before swallowing it like a big girl. "Damn, I like that shit right there, ma."

"Keep fuckin' me like that and you'll see what other tricks I got up my sleeve," she voiced and winked. I laid down on the bed and pulled her in my arms.

Shawty was hood as fuck. That was no denying. But a nigga like me knew I needed someone like her in my corner. There were about to be a lot of changes in this street shit, so having her around was going to be a plus. She was a hood chick, but she was my hood chick. I just hoped her ass was ready for this ride.

## ✣  7  ✣

## HASSAN (SAN)

"Where did you come from?" Fantasy looked up at me and asked.

"My boy told me you were in trouble, so I pulled up. You thought I was going to let my woman and child sit out here needing help? You got me fucked up," I told her.

"Who are you? I don't even know your name," she said.

"Hassan. My name is Hassan. You can call me San like everyone else does."

"I'm not everybody else, Hassan. Why are you pushing up on me so much? You don't know me or a damn thing about me."

"Chill out, ma. I hope the fuck you don't think a nigga out here desperate. I liked what I saw when I saw your ass at the club. I'm just trying to get to know you. If it's that big of a problem, let me know now and I can bounce. I'm not in the business of chasing no-damn-body."

"I didn't ask you to chase me," she snapped, rolling her eyes at me. Nothing annoyed me more than a woman with a fucked-up attitude for no reason. She was really pushing her luck with me.

"Fuck this shit. I'm not 'bout to deal with your attitude. Find somebody else to help you," I snarled.

"I had somebody, but you and your big-body ass friend just took her away from me. What kinda shit is that?"

"He took his woman home because of the time. I'm trying to get your ass out of here, but you trippin'. You got a whole son in your arms that needs a bed and you out here bitchin' about the person trying to help you. I'm not going to hurt yo' lil' ass. If I was, I would have done it by now. Now, get the fuck out the car and let's go," I demanded. I was sick of her shit. There was no other option but for me to put my fuckin' foot down. She stared at me for a while before finally getting out of the car. She must've realized that her ass really didn't have any other choice.

"What about my car?"

"We'll get everything out of it, and it's over. You might as well say goodbye to this car now," I told her. Her face dropped, and I could understand that. It was probably the first car she ever acquired, so it meant something to her. But I had to assume it was hot right now and so was she. I was sure she was running for a reason, and being in that car wasn't going to do her any good.

"What about my bags?"

"You aren't listening to me, I see. We will get everything that you have out of the car before we destroy it. Relax, I got you," I stated.

When we got inside of my car, she got in the backseat with her son. I was perfectly fine with that because she didn't know me, and it was her job as a mother to protect him. If some shit did pop off, she would be close enough to him to react and try to protect him at the same time.

Every now and then, I glanced up in the rearview mirror and could see her staring at me.

"Fantasy?" I called out to her.

"Huh?" she replied.

"You want to tell me what your real name is? Especially since I gave you mine."

"Oh, yeah. Sorry," she apologized. "Fantasy is my stage name."

"For obvious reasons," I stated, and she smiled. She tried to hide the fact that she was blushing, but I could clearly see it.

"My real name is Nakosha, but I go by KoKo," she informed me.

"Okay, cool."

"Where are we going?"

"I'm taking you back to my house so you can be comfortable and safe. Is that cool with you?"

"Yeah, that's fine I guess," she told me. That was the last thing she said to me for the remainder of the ride.

Continuously, I would look up in the rearview mirror to check her out. KoKo was fine as fuck. She had to be about five feet five with full C-cup breasts, a big fat ass, and thick ass thighs. That was exactly how I liked my women. She was the color of Hershey's chocolate with brown eyes and curly hair that hung a little past her shoulders. Her beauty was natural. Other women could never compete with her in my opinion. One look at her, and a man would be crazy to go after another woman. Hell, who wanted a fuckin' snack when you had the whole damn entrée? That was the only thing I could think when I looked at her. She was blessed in all the right places, so I knew God spent a little extra time when he was creating her. She was many thin layers dripping of chocolate, and I wanted to experience each layer.

"Why you staring at me like that?" she asked.

"No reason at all. Does it bother you that I'm checking you out?"

"Checking me out is one thing but staring at me is something completely different. I promise ain't shit changed about me since the last time you looked at me," she snapped.

"Your mouth is going to get you fucked up," I told her.

"By who?" she asked. There was no need for me to respond to her because I was going to say some shit that would have her

48

mother rethinking life. If she knew like I knew, KoKo's ass had better learn fast that I wasn't the nigga to come for unless I sent for you.

It wasn't long before we'd arrived at my house in Gluckstadt. I felt biblical with forty acres and a mule. It really wasn't that much to me, but it was a mansion to anyone else. I pulled under the garage, being sure to close it back behind me before I unlocked the garage door. I assisted KoKo and her son inside the house. Her eyes got big as hell as she admired where I was living.

"This is amazing. I've never seen anything like this in my life," she cooed as she started moving around the house on her own. When she reached the living room, she put her son down on the couch and proceeded to walk through the rest of the house. I kept going back and forth to the car getting everything she had out and taking it up to the room that she was supposed to be staying in.

"Nakoshaaaaaa..." I called out to her when I was done.

"I'm right here. Why are you yelling?" she replied, walking up behind me.

"My bad. I didn't see you. Come on so I can show you where you will be staying," I told her and directed her toward the guest room. Once I showed her where she'd be staying, I showed her another room and told her that her son could stay in there.

"Why would you separate us?" she asked me.

"I just thought maybe you wanted some privacy. Does he sleep with you at home?"

"No. He has his own room. He's three, but he's smart for his age, and he's not afraid of anything. I gave him his own room so he could gain a little independence. Plus, I didn't want my son to grow up thinking it was okay for him to stay in the bed with me until he's ten or eleven like most kids liked to do," she explained.

"That's fine, ma. You don't have to explain all of that to me. It was really just a yes-or-no question. But I get it. How old is he?"

"You don't listen, do you?"

49

"My bad, ma. I was too busy checking you out," I admitted, licking my lips in the process.

"He's three and you can stop all of that. You not about to get any pussy from me," she bellowed.

"If I wanted the pussy, I would've gotten the pussy. Trust me." I winked at her and she blushed again before dropping her head. She became quiet for a brief moment. She didn't say anything further until she could form a serious expression on her face.

"He's three, and he's my everything. I hate that I'm having to put him through this."

"That's not your fault, ma. I can tell that you're a great mother. You're doing the best that you can to help him, but there's only so much you can do. I'm not trying to be funny, but a woman can't raise a man. You shouldn't have to do this alone."

"Who said I was doing this alone?"

"You got a man?"

"Yeah, I ha..." She stopped speaking and dropped her head again. Her dropping her head started to get on my nerves. That made me think she lacked confidence and I didn't need that. I was a cocky mufucka at times and any woman that I was with needed to have that same mentality. She needed to believe that she was un-fuck-wit-able.

"Stop droppin' your damn head. Look a nigga square in the eye. Ain't nobody 'bout to fuck with you now or ever again. Believe me when I say that I got you. Now, tell me what the problem is, ma," I placed my hand under her chin and lifted it back up.

"I had a man. I don't want to talk about all of that right now. His father has been in his life, and that's all that matters."

"I understand." That was all I could say since I felt like I'd stuck my foot in my mouth. "I'm going to get myself ready for bed. You do what you have to do for you and lil' man. The sheets are fresh on both beds. The bathrooms are clean and fully stocked with whatever you need. If you need me, I'm the last bedroom down the hall on the right. Good night," I told her.

"Wait... I have food in my bags," she said.

"And?"

"And I need to put it in the refrigerator before it spoils. I don't want to have to buy food all over again."

"Hol' up. You must've lived with that nigga. Why you take the food out the refrigerator."

"First of all, he lived with me. His punk ass was too lazy to work. I wasn't leaving my food in there to satisfy him. His stomach could drop through his ass for all I care."

"That was petty as fuck." I laughed. "Damn, I know not to piss you off. You'll probably take the damn sockets out of the wall or my fuckin' blinds or some shit," I chuckled.

"Naw. I'd probably just set your damn house on fire," she said with a straight face and then she started to giggle. I stopped laughing because that shit wasn't funny. She seemed crazy enough to do that shit. "I was just playing. I wouldn't do that to you. Just don't hurt me. I can't afford to be hurt again."

"I won't hurt you. I promise. You might as well throw all that food away. I'm sure I have everything you need and whatever I don't have, I'll buy it." I wasn't trying to boast, but I didn't want anything she was bringing from another nigga.

"Why? Are you saying my food isn't good enough?"

"No. I'm saying I don't want anything that you had with another nigga."

"Wait... You want me to be yours right?"

"At some point, you will be. Not right now though because your mouth too fuckin' smart." I told her not right now, but she was already mine.

"Let me give you something to think about," she paused. "This pussy once belonged to another nigga. So did this heart and this body. You just said you didn't want anything I was bringing from another nigga. That must mean you really don't want me because I'd have to bring all of me."

51

Before I knew it, I was in KoKo's face. My face was scrunched up and I was mad as hell. It was hard for me to understand why she would say some stupid shit like that to me. There my goofy ass was trying to help her, and she wanted to be a bitch.

"You're right. I'm going to do us both a favor. Go ahead and put your lil' food up. Get you a good night's rest and in the morning, I'm going to take you to get whatever you had out of your old crib and get you a new one. I'm also going to take you to get another car. After that, you can do whatever the hell you want. Ungrateful bitch!" I grumbled and exited the room without saying another word.

It was clear to me that KoKo was young and had been through a lot at such a young age. I wanted her, but maybe it wasn't the right time for me to put her into my world. I made up in my mind that, after tonight, I was going to help her get on her feet and leave it at that. Whatever she needed, I had no problem helping her with. There was no way I could be with her though. She wasn't ready for my world and her mouth was reckless as fuck. I couldn't see myself dealing with that on a daily basis.

## 8

## NAKOSHA (KOKO)

M aybe I was wrong for the things I said to Hassan, but I didn't completely trust him. He was a man and every man in my life had hurt me. What made him any different?

I'd be a fool to say I wasn't appreciative of the things he'd done for me. He didn't know me, but he still went out of the way to help me. In the back of my mind, I figured the only reason he was really helping me was because he thought he was going to get some pussy. I was a stripper, but that didn't mean shit. Stripping, for me, was the only thing that was keeping my bills paid and the most convenient job I could find that would allow me to continue to be in school and be able to spend time with my son.

Watching Tamir sleep, I was mad at myself because I didn't do a better job at picking who I laid down with. Nate would not be his father. But I was young and dumb. That can't be changed now, and there was really no reason for me to regret it because that would mean I regretted having my son, and that would never be the case for me.

"You good?" Hassan knocked on the door, removing me from my thoughts. I couldn't help but look him up and down because he was definitely a fine specimen of a man.

Hassan stood to be about six feet four and had dreads

hanging a little past the middle of his back. He had a thick ass goatee that I would love to run my clit across to get to his lips that were full and thick. He licked his lips quite often, like he was LL Cool J. After all the licking he was doing, I might as well had changed my name to super soaker because my panties were soaking wet. His skin was the color of caramel, and he had these dark-brown eyes that could quickly draw anyone in. He was the type of man that commanded the attention of anyone in the room without having to open his mouth to say a single word. The brother was fine. Then he had the nerve to be muscular and tattooed damn near from head to toe, as far as I could see.

Hassan had since gotten comfortable. He went from wearing a T-shirt that hugged his biceps and some jeans, to wearing nothing but some Polo boxers. His dick print was clearly visible. That nigga was packing major wood. I started licking my lips, thinking about him being inside of me, even though sex was never insinuated as something he wanted from me.

"Hellooooo... I asked if you were good," he repeated, removing me from my thoughts once again.

"My bad. Yeah, I'm good," I told him. "I take it you aren't mad at me anymore."

"I'm cool off you," he stated and that hurt a little. I didn't mean to make him mad.

"I'm sorry. I didn't mean to be a bitch to you," I apologized.

"It's all good."

"You're saying that, but you don't mean it. You won't even look at me. How you gon' tell me earlier that I needed to look someone in the eye and you're not even following your own advice." I stood from where I was by Tamir's bed and looked at him.

"You're right," he said and stared into my eyes. "I'm cool off you. I'm not mad. I heard what you said, and I'm done with it. Like I said, I'm going to make sure you're straight tomorrow and that's the end of it."

"Oh, so now you don't want me anymore?"

"I'm not doing this with you. I'm tired and all I want is my bed. Are you good?" he said in a rasping tone.

"Yeah, I was just watching him sleep," I said just above a whisper. I felt defeated.

"That's cool and all, but you need to be getting some rest."

"I am." He turned to walk away, but I stopped him when I asked, "Don't you want to know what happened?"

"Naw. You'll tell me when you want me to know."

"He cheated on me. He had another bitch in my house while my son was there." No matter how strong I tried to be, I couldn't. The tears started to freely flow down my face as I explained to him the events that led to me being with him at this very moment.

Hassan came and picked me up and carried me to the guest bedroom he told me to sleep in.

"It's going to be okay, ma," he assured me.

"No, it's not. He's going to make sure I go to jail for shooting at him, and he's going to try to take my son."

"I'm not going to let that happen. Stop worrying your pretty little head with that shit. I got you, ma."

"Why are you helping me?" I asked.

"Because I want to. I saw something in you that I liked," he said.

"But you don't even know me," I voiced again.

"You don't have to keep saying that to me. I really wanted to get to know," he stated.

"Why you keep talking in past tense? Saw? Wanted? What's that about?" I probed.

"It's nothing. I'm just trying to help you, KoKo," he honestly spoke.

"Don't think I'm 'bout to sleep with you because you're helping me. I know all about people saying a shoulder to cry on becoming a dick to ride on, and I'm not about to ride on shit," I freely spoke.

"That's perfectly fine with me. I know it'll be a matter of

time before you're in need, so I'm good. Just make sure you take care of lil' man, and we good. Now, get some sleep. You have a long day tomorrow." When he said that, I felt a little better. It made me think he still wanted me. He couldn't see it, but I was smiling on the inside. Maybe I didn't mess up my chances of us being together after all.

"A long day?"

"Yeah. You have to go quit your job, you have to clean out your crib, and we have to go get you another car."

"Hassan, I need you to understand that I wasn't trying to be mean to you earlier, but I'm just getting out of a relationship. I don't want to rush into another one. I have so much that I want to accomplish in life, and I can't allow anyone to stop me from accomplishing those things," I told him.

"Say no more." That was the last thing he said before he got up and left the room. The way he looked showed me that I'd hurt his feelings, and that was never my intention. At the same time, I had to do what was best for me.

Nate and I had been together for what seemed like forever. We had a child together. Us breaking up was bittersweet because I never would've expected him to hurt me the way that he did. I had a lot of soul-searching to do, and until I could, there was no way I was ready to be in a relationship with anyone else.

# 9

## NATE

*wo Days Later...)*

KoKo was out of her fuckin' mind if she thought I was going to let her leave me without putting up a fight. Then she had the nerve to take her gun out and shoot it like she was trying to kill my ass. I meant too much for her to do that shit, so I didn't know why she was tripping. If she wasn't working so much and gave me the time and attention that I wanted and desired, then there wouldn't have been time for me to allow another woman in to occupy my time. She didn't understand that shit.

When she left last night, I went back inside the apartment. I was going to give her time to cool off and come back home to me. When I noticed that she'd left her money, I grabbed it and left. She was going to have to come looking for it at some point, right? That would lead her back to me, and she wasn't getting a dime back until she agreed that we could work things out. She was my fuckin' cash cow. There was no way I was going to let her get off that easy. Especially not with taking my son with her.

It had been two days since I'd been at the apartment. I went back to see if KoKo decided to bring her ass back home. It wasn't like she had anywhere else to go. Her grandmother was sick, and her parents would never allow her to go there. Her parents were still upset with her for getting pregnant at such a young age, so they weren't really fuckin' with her. She really had nobody but her friend Kita to help her. I'd gone by Kita's house and hadn't seen either of their asses, and I was told that she didn't even go in to work at the club last night. Something was up. I was extremely worried that something may have happened to her. That wouldn't have been good at all for me.

"If you're lookin' for your bitch, she hadn't been home since yesterday and I don't think she's coming back," Michelle's loud as snatched her door open and said.

"Where she go?" I asked.

"You know damn well I don't fuck with her like that and she don't fuck with me. All I know is that she came here with some fine ass man and these other dudes, and they got whatever she wanted out the apartment. I tried to get her to hook me up with one, but she kept laughing. I didn't think the shit was funny."

"Fine man? What the fuck are you talking about? She don't even know anybody else really."

"Well, she looked very close to his ass. Maybe she was cheating on you like you were cheating on her. You know my girl Linette King wrote that book *Don't Cry, Cheat Back*. Maybe she listened to that advice because I would've done that to your dirty dog ass. You know you not shit."

"Michelle, shut the fuck up and go back inside. I don't want to hear none of that shit you talking."

"Why? You don't want to hear the truth that your perfect little angel was probably slinging her pussy at them niggas at the club and she done finally found one that was ready to snatch her off the pole?" She started laughing as she went back in her apartment and shut the door behind her. I was furious as hell. Everything that Michelle said started to make sense to me. Maybe that was the reason KoKo was so quick to say it was over instead of fighting for us.

"Son of a bitch," I yelled as I kicked the door.

Finally opening it, I walked inside. Nothing seemed to be out of place as far as the furniture went. However, I noticed all of the electronics were gone and all the food in the cabinets and refrigerator were gone. I pulled my phone out of my pocket and attempted to call her. For some reason, it kept going straight to voicemail. Each time I thought about what Michelle had said, I became angrier and angrier. So I went to see what else Michelle knew.

*Knock... Knock... Knock...*

"Who is it?" she called out.

"It's Nate. Open the door," I hollered.

"What do you want?" From hearing her voice, it sounded like her ass was standing right behind the door.

"Look, I'm not trying to play games with you, Michelle. All I want to know is what you know about this nigga my girl showed up with."

"Oh, you mean San's fine ass."

"Who?"

"Hassan. The mufuckin' B-O-S-S in these streets. That nigga got everything in Jacktown on lock. Even your bitch." I could hear her laugh.

*Bam...*

Without thinking, I kicked her door. I kicked it so hard that the bitch flew open. Michelle went flying back toward the wall.

"Cheap ass doors," I muttered.

"What the fuck? I'm calling the police, Nate," she stated before rubbing her head.

"You not doing shit but telling me what the fuck you know about this San nigga," I muttered.

"I told you what I know about him. That nigga runs these streets. Everybody who's anybody knows about him."

"If he runs the streets, then how come I don't know about his mufuckin' ass?"

"Because you and your lame bitch don't do shit or go anywhere. All you do is stay in the house, and when you're out, you're too busy chasing pussy to notice what's going on around you. All that bitch does is goes to work, goes to school, and come home."

"Fuck all that. How the hell can I find him?"

"Looking for him is not your best bet unless you want to die. Leave that nigga where he is. Let that bitch be great."

Hearing her say that did something to me. Without thinking, I grabbed her shirt and yoked her ass up. She was pinned up against the wall with no-damn-where to go.

"Let me fuckin' go!" she hollered. I tuned her ass out and wrapped both of my hands around her throat. I started choking and shaking her as if she was a rag doll.

"Oh my God, Nate! What the fuck are you doing?" The sound of KoKo's voice took me out of the trance I was in. I dropped Michelle on the ground and ran over to KoKo. Without giving her a chance to say anything, I wrapped my arms around her and hugged her as if it were the last time I was ever going to see her. "Put me down," she ordered. Even though I didn't want to, I did because I knew it was the best option for me at that point. Especially if I wanted her to talk to me.

"Where have you been? I was worried sick about you," I honestly spoke.

"None of that matters. What matters is where my money is," she retorted.

"Come on and I'll show you," I told her.

Grabbing her hand, I led her over to our apartment. The door was still open from when I opened it earlier hoping she was there. I closed the door behind us and continued to lead her inside. I took her over to the couch and assisted her with taking a seat.

"KoKo, I love you. I took you for granted, and I'm sorry. I didn't sleep with that girl though."

"It doesn't matter if you did or didn't. You disrespected me in the worst way when you allowed her to enter our home. I paid all the bills here while you did nothing but fuss about any and everything. You were the man in our relationship and was supposed to be taking care of me, but you didn't. It was as if I were the one walking around with the dick. You didn't care about me. All you cared about was what you could get out of me. Well, those days are long gone. You can have this apartment, and she can have you."

"What are you saying?"

"We are over with, Nate. I stuck with your ass all these years, and for what? For you to hurt me the way that you did? You made a fool out of me."

"Baby, I didn't fuck her though."

"But you would have. If I wouldn't have come home when I did, you would've slid off in that bitch so fast that even God wouldn't have seen it coming. It's a shame because I was good to you."

"Who is he?"

"Who is who?"

"Who is this San nigga I heard you were with? Were you cheating on me?"

"You have no right to question me about what I do or who I'm with. I'm no longer any business of yours, so it's best if you stay away from me. When I go see the people about child support, I'll let them come up with a visitation schedule for you and Tamir."

"Child support? What the fuck you gonna put me on child support for when I don't have a job?"

"It doesn't matter if you have a job or not. Tamir is still just as much your responsibility as he is mine. So I suggest you find a job and quick because the government is not going to allow you to skirt by without caring for him. You fine and all, but I don't think you want bitches seeing your face plastered all over one of those fuckin' billboards for not taking care of your child."

KoKo stood up to leave, but I wasn't ready for her to go. I stood up along with her and reached for her, but she pulled away from me. That was not something I was used to, nor did I like it.

"Where's my money, Nate?"

"It's in the bedroom. Come with me to get it," I instructed her.

"Naw, I'll stay here while you go get it," she quipped.

"Why can't you go to the room with me?" I probed, raising an eyebrow.

"Because I don't trust you. I'm not about to put myself in any more danger than I'm already in," she stated.

"I've never hurt you. Why would you think I'd do it now?" I pondered.

"I saw you choking the life out of Michelle. If you'd do it to her, you'd do it to me. I'm not risking it. The only real reason I came back was because I left some of Tamir's baby books here. When they get ready to evict your ass for not paying the rent, I don't want to lose his books in the process," she admitted. That shit hurt me.

"So you saying you not gonna make sure the bills are paid so I can keep a roof over my head?"

"Can elephants fly? You have got to be smoking some good shit to think I would continue to finance your ass while you do what you want with the next bitch. Aht aht... Try that shit with somebody else," she rattled off.

"Fuck you, KoKo. You ain't shit but a stripper hoe anyways. You think you look good because you work at the fuckin' strip club? Bitch, you wasn't shit when you started, and you won't be shit when you stop. That's my mufuckin' money," I barked. She'd pissed me off to the max. She wasn't getting one red cent until she told me that she was going to work on our relationship with me. The bitch had me fucked up.

"That's fine too," she said just above a whisper. I stood back and watched as she entered Tamir's room and came back out a few seconds later with a small bag. I was sure it was the bag that contained his baby books. I attempted to take the bag from her, but she jerked back so fast that I went sliding down to the floor.

When I got up to try to take the bag from her again, KoKo darted out the fuckin' door. I chased behind her but quickly stopped when I noticed a couple of big ass niggas standing outside by a SUV. I assumed that was the Hassan nigga that Michelle was telling me about.

"We got a problem? Why you running?" he asked KoKo when she neared him. Looking back at me, she shook her head as if she were telling him she was running for no reason. He glanced up at me like he wanted to say something but stopped when KoKo wrapped her arms around his neck.

Standing in the breezeway, I watched on in awe as KoKo got in the car with the nigga and they pulled away. That shit hurt me to my heart. I'd never been so hurt or embarrassed before in my life. I took my ass back inside the apartment we once shared feeling defeated. Something had to be done. There was no way our relationship was over just like that.

## ❧ 10 ❧

## NAKITA (KITA)

*(One Month Later...)*
It had been a month since I met Major, and I could honestly say he was everything I could've asked for and more. Some people would probably say it was too soon for me to be saying that, but in my opinion, when you know... you know. He made me put my dancing shoes down, and I had no problem doing so as long as he agreed to take care of me. I had a few bills stacked, so I wasn't hurting for anything. However, I still picked up another job because I didn't want to solely depend on him for everything.

"You ready for your sponge bath, Mr. James?" I asked one of my elderly patients. I went through this fly-by-night training course to become certified as a CNA and got a job at Pleasant Hills Nursing Home. It didn't take long for me to get in, because the administrator remembered my mother.

"No," he shouted.

"What's wrong, Mr. James?" I asked like I really gave a damn. He was the hardest patient that I had, which was why I always waited until it was time for me to leave before I dealt with his old grumpy ass.

"I don't want you touching me. I want the nurse with the big booty to come in here." Mr. James was also a pervert. Everybody hated working with him. That was why when Rob was working, we always let him deal with Mr. James. Just my luck, Rob's ass called in sick today. I bet wasn't shit wrong with his ass.

"Okay, that's fine. I can't make you do a damn thing," I snapped. I was sick of his shit. It was the end of the day. I was tired and ready to go home. He wasn't about to work my nerves for the remainder of my time there.

Leaving out of the room, I went up to the nurse's station to let them know what was going on. I was told that I needed to go back in there and clean Mr. James, even if he didn't want me to. Of course, I wasn't trying to hear that shit, so I stepped inside the break room to call Major.

"Hey, ma," he answered on the second ring.

"Hey, baby! What you doing?" I queried.

"Nothing. 'Bout to go into a meeting. What's up?" he asked.

"I'm debating on whether or not I should walk out of here. These mufuckas keep pissing me off," I voiced to him.

"Calm down, ma. What's going on with you?" One thing I could say about Major was that he knew how to calm me down quicker than anybody else that I knew. Even KoKo, and she'd been my best friend for years. It was something about his voice that really made me feel like everything was going to be okay.

"I'm just over working for these people. I don't want to depend on you when we've only been together for a month, and I know you aren't going to allow me to go back to stripping."

"Absolutely not. I branded that pussy. Them niggas saw it before, but I'd be damned if they're ever going to see it again," he barked. I giggled to myself because I knew how serious he was about it. In fact, he took me the very next day to the club to make me clean my shit out. I had to burn all of the clothes I used to wear on stage. Shit, I was shocked he let me keep the money that I made. When he said he wanted me to distance myself from that old lifestyle, his ass was not playing at all.

"Okay, baby. I get it. I just don't want to do this."

"I don't know why you took your lil' ass in there anyways. You knew damn well you didn't want to be wiping them old people's asses. Then be coming to my shit trying to rub all up on me. Be smelling like piss and shit." He chuckled causing me to giggle.

"Don't do me. You know I don't ever smell when I get around you." I giggled some more.

"You do. I just don't be saying nothing to save your feelings. You be smelling like a whole geriatric patient yourself. Shitty ass. I'ma start calling you pisty for smelling pissy and shitty." He was killing himself laughing.

"Fuck you." I couldn't help but laugh with him because he was retarded as hell. "Let me get off this phone. I'll be clocking out in a few."

"Awwww... daddy's lil' working girl," he teased.

"Shut up, clown," I joked.

"A'ight, ma. You still coming to the party tonight?"

"You know I am. Does he know that you're throwing this party for him?" Him would be Hassan. He was turning twenty-five, so Major was throwing this big ass birthday bash for him. It was my job to make sure KoKo got there.

KoKo stayed with Hassan for two days. In that time, he got her a new apartment, helped her get what she wanted out of her old apartment, and made her quit the club. He paid her tuition so she could finish out school and left her with some other money to help her survive for the next few months. He told her that whenever she needed something, all she had to do was hit him up and he'd do whatever he could to help her. She didn't understand why he stopped pursuing her the way that he did when they first met, but she never questioned him.

"Naw. He has no idea. The nigga been snoopin' and shit trying to find out what's up, but I told everybody if they opened their mouths, I was taking their ass out. San has been doing everything for everybody. It's time for somebody to do something for him."

"That's very sweet of you, baby. He's lucky to have you in his life."

"Naw. I'm the lucky one. San has done more for me than anybody else in my life. I owe him my life. You just make sure you're there and you bring KoKo's crazy ass. My boy needs her in his life, even though she's ratchet as fuck. Y'all are some of the hoodest women I've ever met in my life." He chuckled.

"Whatever. We are just as hood as y'all are. Be glad y'all got women that'll ride for y'all."

"I got a woman that'll ride for me, and San needs the same. You need to get your girl to stop trippin' and give my guy some play," he muttered.

"Trust me, she's not the reason they're not together," I snapped.

"Ma, it's definitely her. Don't turn your face up if you see him with another chick on his arm," he advised.

"If that nigga rolls up in that party with another bitch, you better make sure she scats because he is leaving that bitch with KoKo. I promise I'll drag that hoe out of there by her hair."

"Calm down, killa. We'll work it out. Just be there and be on time and make sure KoKo looks nice."

"A'ight, baby. I'll see you tonight," I told him and ended the call.

Before I stepped out of the break room to go back to enter-tain Mr. James's ass, I hit KoKo up. I needed to make sure she was going to have her ass ready for tonight. She needed to be the first one at the party after all of the things Hassan had done for her.

"Hello," she answered, sounding tired.

"Hey, girl! What's up with you?"

"Nothing. Just put Tamir down for his nap."

"Are you ready for tonight? I need you dressed to the nines because Hassan is going to need you lookin' good standing by his side."

"Girl, please! Hassan not worried about me. I haven't heard

from his ass in over a month. I'm only going to keep you company, and don't think I'm staying long."

"Eww... Don't show up with that attitude. Now be at my house for six so we can roll out by seven."

The party actually didn't start until ten, but I needed her to come to my place early because Major was sending someone over to do our hair and makeup. He was also sending someone over with several different outfits for us to choose from. We were going to need every bit of those four hours to get ourselves together.

"Whatever. Bye, girl!" She hung up the phone without giving me the chance to respond.

"Bitch," I said to myself as I slid my phone back in my pocket. Sticking my head out of the break room, I checked to see if anyone was watching me before finally leaving out of the room. I made my way back down to where Mr. James was. He was sitting in his wheelchair, watching a rerun of *Family Feud*. He was laughing loud as hell.

It was clear that he wasn't trying to take a bath, and it was even clearer that I wasn't about to force him. I'd leave that up to the next shift. Pulling out the extra chair that was in his room, I put it right next to him and took a seat. If I couldn't get his ass to do what I wanted him to do, I'd just join his ass until it was time for me to leave.

## 🦋 II 🦋

## NAKOSHA (KOKO)

"**B**itch, what the fuck is taking you so long? I thought you said the party started at seven," I fussed at Kita's ass.

When I got off the phone with her earlier, I decided to lay down and take a nap while Tamir was sleeping. When we finally woke up, I realized that I was running late, so I tossed on the first thing I could find. By the time I was done, Nina, the girl Major hired to babysit Tamir, was knocking on the door. I told her very clearly how I didn't fuck around when it came to my son and if I found one hair out of place when I got back to him, she would not see the light of day again. I meant that shit. I played about a lot of fuckin' things, but my son wasn't one of those things.

"Who the hell you know shows up at a party on damn time?" she hollered as she stepped out of the bathroom. She was still taking the rollers out of her damn head. Shit was aggy.

"It's a surprise party, hoe. That means we have to be there before he gets there," I sassed.

"What you on? You in a big hurry to see your man, I see," she joked.

"Girl, please, he is not my man. I ain't got my ass on him like he don't have his ass on me. He fine, but he not fine enough for me to be chasing him around like I'm some sick puppy or some shit," I fussed.

"Whatever. I'm not trying to hear that. We both know that you want San's ass. That's why you always get in your feelings when I talk about him." There was no need to respond because what she said was one hundred percent the truth.

Kita sashayed back inside of the bathroom without a care in the world. I flopped across her bed and pulled my phone out of my bra. Unlocking it, I went straight to my Facebook app. I went to the last picture I posted on my page and rolled my eyes. Nobody couldn't tell me I wasn't fine as fuck, but I had some hating ass friends. They'd like other people's shit but wouldn't like mine. I wasn't even sure why they wanted to be my friend if they weren't going to comment or like shit. *Might as well delete their asses and make room for my real fans*, I thought to myself as I laughed.

"What's so funny?" Kita came out of the bathroom and asked.

"I'm over here tripping out on Facebook," I replied.

"Why? Somebody did something stupid again?" she queried.

"Naw. I'm just trippin' on how people stay your friends to be nosy but ain't never got shit to say to you."

"Girl, Facebook is based off popularity. I've come to realize that."

"Says the person that gets over three hundred likes on everything she posts."

"You a lie," she remarked and started laughing.

"You laughing because you know I'm telling the truth. You could post 'I shitted on myself', and the bullshit would more than likely go viral." I giggled. She couldn't say shit because she knew I was telling the truth.

Kita waltzed right back into the bathroom, where she remained for another thirty minutes. I'd gotten sleepy and was ready to pass out on the bed. I'd already had a long day and was ready to go to sleep. I hated that I even agreed to go to his party. It wasn't really my scene, because of all the bougie people I knew were going to be in the building. Major and Hassan were street niggas, but they carried themselves in a professional manner at all times. Even when they were about to fuck some shit up, people knew to take them seriously because they were certainly a force to be reckoned with.

When people looked at me, they automatically had me pegged as ratchet, and I was fine with that. You know why? Because they knew not to fuck with me. You could look at me wrong, and I was ready to fight. It was the way I grew up. My grandmother was like that until she got sick. My mother was like that until my father became a pastor and she decided she wanted to be a social worker. Hell, all of the women in my family were like that. We didn't play games. You were either going to respect us or be dealt with. It was your choice. I was the true definition of being a product of my environment.

Standing up, I walked over to her mint-colored floor-length mirror that I'd purchased for her from Walmart for her birthday last year. She thought it was the best gift ever, when I only paid six dollars for it. It was the thought that counted. It was purchased because she was so in love with herself. She couldn't walk past a mirror without stopping to check herself out. That included the mirrors on the car. She had to stop. There was no denying that my friend was bad as fuck though.

In my opinion, Kita was very shapely. She really had a Coke bottle-shaped body, and she stayed in the gym, making sure her shit was tight and right. I envied that about her. People always told me how beautiful I was, but her shit was done effortlessly. She could eat anything she wanted and still be small. I felt like I had to run a marathon if I even looked at anything sweet. Thinking about food reminded me that I hadn't eaten anything all day. Kita's ass needed to hurry up so we could stop and grab something on the way to the damn party in case the food there was nasty.

"I'm ready," Kita finally announced, stepping out of the bathroom wearing a damn robe.

"What the fuck? Where are you going with that?" I asked. She was out of her mind if she thought she was going anywhere with me wearing a robe. Major was not about to kill me fuckin' with her ass.

"Calm down, girlie. Major set something up for us. Go in the bathroom and put the other robe on very quickly," she instructed me.

"Set something up like what? Why I gotta get out of my clothes when I'm already dressed to go?" I fired question after question off at her, wondering why the hell she had an issue with what I wanted to wear. I thought I looked fine.

"You not going anywhere with me looking like you just went shopping at the Salvation Army. All that damn money we made at the club and that San gave you, and this was the best outfit you could come up with. You've got to be kidding me," she chided. "Go in the bathroom and put the robe on."

Hesitantly, I did as she said. By the time I'd gotten completely undressed and came back out of the bathroom, her bedroom was filled with several different people.

"Who the hell are they?" I asked her.

"Major set this up for us. It's like a mini pampering session. We are going to get our hair and makeup done and then we have someone here that's going to dress us. This is going to be so fun," she announced, clapping her hands. I couldn't remember the last time I saw her get this damn excited.

It took us a good two and a half hours to get our hair done. Mine was pinned up in a beautiful bun. I went through all the clothes trying to find something classy to wear. Kita must've gotten tired of me being so indecisive because she came over to me and handed me a beautiful red dress with gold rhinestones and a slit up the left side of it. The dress was bad as hell.

"Here, put this on," she instructed me.

"Why you telling me to put it on? Why the hell didn't you

wear it?" I questioned her because of how beautiful the dress was.

"I have my reasons for not putting it on. Now, stop being so damn complicated and put the damn dress on," she ordered.

Pouting, I stomped inside the bathroom and took the robe off. I admired the dress once more before finally putting it on. There was no denying that I looked like a goddess once I'd changed. Even if I hadn't changed my clothes, I thought I was beautiful as fuck. Kita gave me some gold pumps with rhinestones to wear with the dress, and I found some gold accessories that really set the dress off even more. Kita was dressed in an all-black bodycon dress that hugged her every curve with some black open-toed Jimmy Choo shoes with diamonds all over them.

"Now, this how the fuck you slay an outfit," Kita cooed.

"Hell yeah. We fine as fuck, friend," I stated.

"You think we should get a glass of wine? We need something in our system before we head to the party. You know how your nerves get. Maybe we should hit a blunt or something," she advised.

"Bitch, no, ma'am. It's already late, and you said we had to be there before seven. It's almost ten. Major is going to kill us."

"Naw, the party starts at ten. We have to be there by 10:30 because that's when he told Hassan to be there. I just told you to come early so I could surprise you with the pampering. Let's get out of here before we're late for real," Kita stated.

Grabbing our purses, we headed for the door. We decided to ride together because it was late, and it would've been safer. We weren't worried about getting back home because we knew that Major would make sure we got back safely.

Even though I didn't think Hassan would be interested in seeing me, I knew I was fine as fuck. One look at me, and his ass would be falling to my feet. That would be all the validation that I needed that he wanted me as much as I wanted him.

## ❧ 12 ❧

# HASSAN (SAN)

Major kept trying to get me to ride to the club with him, but I wasn't doing all that. When it was time for me to leave, I was getting in my shit and heading out. My mind really wasn't on partying, because I was worried about KoKo. I hadn't heard from her since I moved her into her own apartment. It was true that I put her in a nice setup and made sure she was taken care of, but I really thought that would help her to see how much I was trying to be there for her and maybe that would give her a reason to trust me.

Telling myself that she'd been through too much and that trying to pursue a relationship with her wasn't the best thing right now was the worst advice I could've given myself. She was all I could think about. We could be sitting in an important meeting, and I would be in my own little world thinking about her and her son. Tamir had grown on me in the two days that they were living with me. It made me think about what it would be like if I had a child of my own. I wanted that, and I wanted it with KoKo.

Rocking Gucci from my head down to my feet, I rocked diamonds on my neck, wrist, and both ears. I even had my hair freshly tapered with my dreads pinned up in a neat bun.

It was a little after 10:30 when I finally pulled up in front of the club. There was a line of people standing outside, waiting to get in. Major was standing at the front door speaking to security about something. I stepped out my whip and tossed my key to the valet before approaching Major.

"What's up, nigga? You late," Major grumbled.

"We all know don't shit start until I show up, so there ain't no way I'm late." I chuckled. We dapped each other up before entering the building.

"Surrrrprrriiiseeeee!" people yelled. I looked over at Major and started laughing. He got me good. I definitely wasn't expecting this. Hell, my mind was so consumed with KoKo and what she could've been up to that I didn't even think about my birthday coming up.

"Everybody clap it up for the man of the hour, Hassan. Happy birthday my nigga," DJ Clive stated, holding his glass in the air. That was when two women with the fattest asses I'd ever seen in my life came over and guided me over to the VIP section where there were bottles lined up, ready to be popped.

"I got a surprise for you," Major came over and said in my ear.

"Another one?" I quizzed, wondering what more he could have up his sleeve for me. That was when I spotted her.

KoKo came waltzing into the VIP section with Kita following closely behind her. Kita went over to where Major was, and KoKo came toward me.

"Happy birthday, Hassan," she stated.

"Thank you, ma. How have you been?"

"I've been good."

"What about lil' man?"

"He's fine. He's been asking about you. You should come see him when you aren't busy," she suggested.

"I'm never too busy for him or you," I assured her, winking at her.

"Heyyyyyy, Hassan," a random girl came over to me and

started talking. KoKo's face scrunched up. I knew shit could go left, but I was curious to see how she would handle someone stepping to me.

"So you didn't see me standing here talking to him?" she asked the girl.

"Yeah, but you not his woman, so he's free game," the girl replied.

"Bitch, you got me fucked up. I'll snatch all that shit out of your head if you don't get the fuck on," she snapped.

"Girl, bye! Hassan is single so I can talk to him. Besides, if me talking to him was such a big issue, why didn't he tell me to leave?" Her bringing me into the conversation was what fucked it up for her. I was going to ride with KoKo before any other hoe, so I had to shut her mufuckin' ass down quick.

Opening my mouth to say something, I didn't have time because KoKo grabbed the girl by her hair and yanked her back. The girl went tumbling down to the ground. KoKo started kicking her in the head. I picked her up and moved her around so she wouldn't kill the girl.

"Chill out, ma. You're going to kill her."

"Fuck that bitch! She not about to disrespect me like that. You ain't see me standing there?" she asked me.

"Yeah, I saw you standing there. Hell, I was talking to you," I replied.

"Exactly! Her mufuckin' ass did too. You better tell your hoes not to try me like that," she fumed.

"Damn, ma. Why I gotta have hoes?"

"That's exactly what she is... a mufuckin' hoe. Now, I don't know what the fuck kinda game you think we playing, but you're mine. I've let this shit go on for long enough."

"You let what go on for long enough?"

"This shit where you thought you were playing hard to get. I'm done with it." She placed her finger on my chest and started poking me as she said, "I'll fuck you and these hoes up if you or them ever try to disrespect me again." When she was done, she placed her mouth on top of mine and pinned me up against the wall. We engaged in a long, passionate kiss. It seemed like we were the only people inside the club. I was ready to leave and get her home so I could finally feel the inside of her.

"Lemme get the check. This party is over," I hollered out. Major and Kita looked at me and started laughing.

"Enjoy your party. We'll have plenty of time together, later," she told me.

"Naw. Fuck that! I gotta feel you before you change your mind," I told her. She started laughing, but I was so serious.

"We'll be back," she told Kita and Major and then she took my hand and led me out of the VIP section.

"Where are we going?" I asked.

"Do you have a problem with me taking the lead?" she asked. I shook my head. "Good, then shut up and let's go," she commented.

Doing as she said, I remained quiet and followed her lead. We ended up in the women's bathroom. KoKo tugged at my pants until she was able to get them down and then pushed me down on the toilet. I thought ma was going to give me a lil' head or something, but she didn't. She pulled her dress up, moved her panties to the side, and straddled me.

"Are you sure this is okay?"

"Be spontaneous, baby. Everything between us is not always going to be perfect. Live in the moment. I want some dick, and you want to know how my pussy feels. This is your birthday, so let's enjoy the moment," she stated.

Slowly, KoKo slid down on my dick. I threw my head back because her pussy was tight, hot, and wet. I'd been so consumed with work and thinking about her that it had been a minute since the last time I'd had sex. That meant it was only a matter of time before I shot all of her insides up.

"Fuck, girl," I moaned.

"Your dick is too big," she commented. I plopped my head

back up to look into her eyes. They were closed, and she was twisting her mouth as if she were in too much pain.

Placing my hands on her hips, I stopped her from moving. I knew my dick was big, but I didn't think it would cause her that much pain. It had me wondering how long it had been since she'd been with a man. Either it had been a while, or the last nigga she was with didn't do shit to make sure her pussy was open because the way her face looked proved that she was experiencing excruciating pain, and that was the last thing I wanted her to feel.

"Relax, baby. I'm not trying to hurt you," I told her. "I'd never do that. Take your time and grind on your dick," I directed her. "Rock your hips back and forth and just grind on me, baby."

It wasn't long before KoKo eased up. She rocked back and forth and grinded her pussy around in a circle on my dick. Shit, I was supposed to be writing my name in her pussy, but it seemed like she was spelling her name on my dick. I was getting weak. Hell, I felt like I was going to fall off the damn toilet. The shit was feeling good. My nut was building up quick as hell. I held it for as long as I could because I didn't want it to end. If I could pick her up and remain inside of her until I got her back to my house, I'd fuck the hell out of her for the rest of the night. Since I knew that was impossible, I did the only other thing I could think of doing.

Picking her up, I placed her back against the wall and started stroking deep inside of her. She moaned loud as hell. I could feel her nails as she clawed into my back.

"Damn it, San. Shitttt..." she cried out.

"Say my name."

"San."

"I can't hear that shit."

"San!"

"Naw, say my whole mufuckin' government."

"I can't. I'm about to cum, baby. Why you doing this to me? It's not supposed to feel this fuckin' good," she whined.

"Yes it is, baby. You supposed to feel this shit even when I take my dick out of you," I told her as I started drilling faster inside of her.

"Baby, I'm cumminnn'..." she wailed.

When she said that, I pulled my dick out of her. She shook a little, but she didn't cum.

"What the fuck? Put it back baby. Put it back!!"

"Say please."

"What?"

"Say please or you not gettin' any more of this immaculate dick," I told her, sounding cocky as fuck.

"Put it back, baby. Pleaseeeee put it back," she pleaded with me.

Swiftly, I slid back inside of her and went to work moving in and out of her. I moved up and down and circled my hips around. I watched as her eyes rolled to the back of her head right before she threw her head back.

"Uh huh, that's what the fuck I'm talking about. That's what the fuck I'm talking about. Take this dick, baby. Nut all on your dick."

"Oh my Gawwwddd... I'm about to cummmmm..." she announced once more.

"Me too, baby. Let that shit go, ma," I told her, and as soon as her body started to shake, I felt her muscles tighten around my dick and her juices flowing down it. That was when I let loose and shot everything within me inside of her. I'd had so much built up that when it was finally out, my legs got weak. I thought we were going to hit the floor, but I was able to maneuver back over to the toilet and take a seat with my dick still resting inside of her.

"You felt so good, Hassan," she told me when she was able to regain control of her breathing.

"You did too, baby. I've thought about that from the moment I first laid eyes on you," I truthfully admitted.

"Me too, baby. I'm glad we waited. It was well worth it," she cooed.

"Just wait until I get you home," I told her.

"Oh, I know you are going to fuck my head up when we get home, and I'm cool with that. I just wanted to give you a little sample of what you had been missing," she bragged.

"Whatever. You ready to leave now?"

"No. Let's enjoy your birthday a little longer. I promise it'll be worth the wait," she said before placing another kiss on my lips. It was better than the first time that we kissed.

After a little while longer, we got up and cleaned ourselves up before rejoining the party. She was telling me to enjoy it, but I couldn't. There was only one thing on my mind, and that was getting inside of her again. She'd better have as much fun as she could because once I was done with her ass, she wasn't going to be able to walk right for at least a week.

## ❧ 13 ❧

# MAJOR

Hassan thought his ass was slick. When I saw the way KoKo handled that other broad that tried to step to him, I fell out laughing. I had to keep my hands around Kita's ass because she was ready to attack if KoKo had gotten hit.

"Let's go dance." Kita grabbed my hand and pulled me out on the dance floor. Dancing was not my thing, but I didn't mind standing there and enjoying my lady bouncing her ass on my dick. It was only giving me a preview of what she'd be doing for me later tonight.

Song after song, Kita twerked her ass off. After the second song, a nigga was ready to sit down, but she wasn't ready, and I knew I couldn't leave her on the dance floor by herself. So I thought of something even better. I guided Kita off the dance floor and into the office of the club. It was a club that Hassan and I owned, so we had access to any and everything inside of it.

"We are goin' to get into trouble," she stated when I led her in the office.

"How? This my shit," I told her. Her mouth popped open in awe. "Ma, I'm sure you think the only thing I do is that street shit, but I promise you there's more to me than you know."

"Please don't think I think bad of you, because I don't. I admire everything about you."

"Oh really?"

"Yes, really, silly. Why would I not?"

"Then show me how much," I stated as I picked up a remote off the table and pushed a few buttons. Out of nowhere, a pole started coming down from the ceiling. When it reached the floor, I bent down and locked it into place.

"Who has a pole in their office?" she quizzed.

"Girl, you know your man is a freak," I spoke prior to licking my lips. "Give your man a private show. That's something you've never done."

"No problem, daddy," she happily stated.

Standing back, I watched as Kita checked the pole. As a smile spread across her face, she took ahold of my hand and led me over to a chair that was sitting near the pole. Once I was seated, she pulled out her phone and started looking for a song.

"Play something slow. I want to see you grind on that pole like you grind on this dick," I requested.

*"When we... When we... Mmmm... When we... Go...*

*I like it when you lose it.*

*I like it when you go there.*

*I like the way you use it.*

*I like that you don't play fair.*

*Recipe for a disaster.*

*When I'm just trynna take my time.*

*Stroke is gettin' deep and faster.*

*You're screamin' like I'm outta line..."*

*When We* by Tank began playing in the background. Seductively, Kita swayed her hips from side to side. Instantly, my dick bricked up in my pants as I thought about being inside of her. Everything that she was doing was turning me on. She pulled the straps down on her dress and allowed it to fall to the floor, revealing her perky breasts since she wasn't wearing a bra. Her G-string ran perfectly down her ass cheeks. With her heels still on, she grabbed the pole and climbed it all the way to the top before twisting her body around it and slowly coming down into a split. It made me wish I was at the bottom of the pole, waiting for her to land on my dick.

"Damn, ma," I blurted out about to lose my mind. My dick was jumping in my pants, begging to be set free.

It was five minutes later when I realized I couldn't take it anymore. I had to let my dick breathe. I unbuttoned and unzipped my pants and stood up to let them fall. Kita dropped down to her knees and crawled toward me. Eye level to my dick, she quickly stuffed all of me inside of her mouth. It was evident she was a pro at the shit because she was able to do it with no hands. That wasn't easy for most women to do, but my baby was handling that shit like she was a porn star.

Throwing my head back, I took in her intoxicating scent that fluttered up to my nostrils as she continued to suck and slurp all on my dick. I wanted to taste her so bad, but I wanted her to continue to give me pleasure as well. So I gripped her around the waist, lifted her up, and flipped her to where her pussy would be in my face and my dick would be in hers. I didn't have to say a single word to her. She knew what it was when I yanked her G-string off and buried my face in her pussy. She went back to work sucking on my dick. She would take breaks between licking, slurping, and sucking to moan while I went to work massaging her clit with my tongue.

My tongue was good for more than just talking, and she was finally about to experience that shit. I twisted and twirled my tongue around on her clit before dipping it in and out of her wet pussy.

"Mmmm..." she exhaled. She released my dick from her mouth and grabbed a hold of my knees. "That feels so fuckin' good, baby. Please don't stop," she pleaded with me.

"Tell me you love this shit. Tell me you love me," I stopped long enough to say.

"I love you, Major. I love you more than you'll ever know,"

she confessed. I already knew that because I could see it in her eyes every time we saw each other.

No, we hadn't been together long, but I knew that she gave me this indescribable feeling that I didn't want to lose. It made me feel good and it was something I'd never felt before. Her saying that she loved me only confirmed what I already knew, but it felt good to hear. I just couldn't say it back because I was still unsure of what it was.

"Baby, you're going to make me cum," she added, but I wasn't ready for her to bust yet. I wanted to feel the inside of her, so I flipped her back over and slid her down on my dick. "Mmmm... Sssss..." she hissed.

"Ride this dick, baby. Fuck me like this the last time you'll ever see me," I instructed her.

**Smack... Smack...**

I smacked her on both ass cheeks as she picked up speed. Kita was riding my dick like she was in a rodeo. I tried to slow her down, but it was as if she was resisting my direction and moving at the beat of her own drum. Moving my thumb up to her mouth, I placed it inside and allowed her to suck on it for a while before moving my hand back around to her ass and slowly inserting it inside of her ass.

"Yesss...." she moaned before throwing her head back. I pulled it back forward. I wanted her to look into my eyes while I was pleasuring her.

"Look at me. I want to see you enjoying this dick," I told her as I gazed into her charcoal eyes. I was mesmerized by her beauty. Kita just didn't know what she was doing to me. I removed my finger from her ass and brought it up to my mouth. I sucked on it so she'd know I had no problem tasting every inch of her.

"Damn, baby. You freaky freaky," she said.

With my arms under hers, I placed my hands on her shoulders and pulled her down as I pushed up deeper inside of her. She loudly moaned out and tried to move because of all the pressure I was giving her, but her strength was no match for what I was doing to her.

"Major..." she said my name.

"Yes, baby..."

"You feel so fuckin' good. I don't ever want this to end," she said before she placed her lips on top of mine. We engaged in a passionate kiss as her juices came raining down out of her and onto my dick. The minute I felt her wetting me up, I couldn't hold it any longer. Placing my mouth on her shoulder, I bit down on it as I emptied myself inside of her. "You trying to get me pregnant?" she said out of nowhere.

"I'm not trying to, but if it happened, would it be a bad thing?" She got quiet on me. She even went as far as turning her head away from me. That worried me. Was it that bad to think of possibly having my child? "What's the problem, ma?" I queried.

"It's not bad if I were to get pregnant by you, but we're just getting to know each other. I don't want to sound mean, but I've watched KoKo struggle. She's a great woman with a good head on her shoulders. She deserves so much more than the hand that was dealt to her. I just don't want to end up like that," she confessed.

"Do you think I would leave you with a baby? I'm not that type of nigga, and if you thought that I was, then you really don't know me at all. In fact, how could you claim you love me if you have a thought like that?" I questioned her.

"Wait a minute.... You asked me to tell you that I loved you, but you didn't say it back." I knew her ass was changing the subject, but I didn't say anything.

"Say what back?" I played dumb.

"Tell me that you love me," she quipped.

"I can't say it back," I told her.

"And why can't you?" She probed.

"Because I don't say shit that I don't mean. One thing about me is that I'll always keep shit a buck. If I'm not sure that I love you yet, I can't tell you that I do," I admitted. Her facial expression changed, and she appeared sad.

"Don't," she said as I opened my mouth to speak. "Don't sit here and try to pacify what you just said to me. I get where you're going with this, and it's cool. Let's get back to the party," she muttered.

Kita stood up off me and walked over to the bathroom that was inside the office. She disappeared without saying another word to me. While she was in the bathroom, I used the kitchen area to clean myself up. By the time I'd adjusted my clothes and gotten myself to go back out to the party, she came back out of the bathroom.

"You ready?" I asked. I reached out, ready to lead her out, but she pulled away from me.

Kita had an attitude. One that I was not about to deal with. If she couldn't appreciate the fact that I was being honest with her, that was her problem. One way or another, her ass was going to have to learn that things weren't going to always go her way or be the way she wanted them to be. Kissing people's ass wasn't something that I did, and I sure as fuck wasn't about to start doing the shit now.

## 🎔 14 🎔

## NATE

There were so many people in the club that it didn't take much for me to get lost in the crowd. My eyes remained trained on KoKo and Hassan the entire time they were there. When they went inside the bathroom and stayed gone for a long period of time, I already knew what they were doing. It had my blood boiling because that was something I'd never been able to get KoKo to do with me. She acted like she was too good for freaky shit like that, but she had the time to be freaky with the next nigga. It made me wonder what the fuck else she had been doing that I didn't know about.

"What can I get you?" the bartender asked when I reached the bar.

"Let me get a vodka and orange juice," I told her. I needed something light so I could keep my head clear.

"Hey, good looking," a female came up to me and said. She was very forward, and I didn't like that. Aggressive females weren't my thing, because that meant it would be hard getting them to submit to me.

"'Sup?" I flatly spoke.

"What you mean 'sup? What kind of greeting is that?"

"The only kind of greeting you're about to get out of me. Don't you have somebody else you can bother?"

While she stood in front of me rolling her neck and popping her mouth, I could see KoKo and Hassan emerge from the back of the club. They were holding hands and making googly eyes to each other. The shit was pissing me off more. They were headed my way. There was no way I could let them see me. So, I did the only logical thing I could think of doing by pulling the annoying woman in for a kiss. Surprisingly, she didn't fight it. Turning our bodies so my back would be facing Hassan and KoKo, I continued to kiss the woman. The way we were kissing, you would've thought we were a couple.

My eyes stayed trained up on the mirror that was above the bar. I watched KoKo's every move. Noticing them move towards VIP, I pushed the woman off me.

"Heyyyyyy... What you stop for?" she asked, trying to move back in closer to me. I shook my head and moved away from her. I got as close to the VIP section as I could, hoping I could hear anything they talked about. It would be quite impossible to hear much with the music blasting through the speakers.

It was hard for me to stand by and see KoKo having fun with Hassan. That was something she was supposed to be doing with me. She said we were over, but there was no way I was ready for this relationship to be over. What made her think it was okay for her to make that decision for me? For us?

"I have to go to the bathroom." I made out what she was saying by reading her lips. That was really the only thing I could do.

They had been back in their section for about thirty minutes before she told him she needed to use the bathroom.

"You need me to go with you?" he asked. That made me even madder. He kept pushing up on my girl and that wasn't going to work for me.

"Naw, I got it, baby," she told him before placing a kiss on his cheek and leaving him in the VIP section while she went to the bathroom. Staying a small distance behind her, I made sure to keep my eyes trained on her as I followed her through the crowd toward the bathroom.

KoKo knocked on the door to see if anyone was in there before pushing it open. I studied the area to make sure no one could see me before I pushed inside the bathroom behind her right as she was about to lock the door.

"What the fuck!" she exclaimed with a look of shock on her face.

"I guess this means you weren't expecting to see me here," I taunted.

"No. Now get out so I can use the bathroom," she ordered.

'I'm not doing shit. I've seen every inch of your body and I've been in the bathroom before when you used it. This time ain't no different," I told her. A smirk appeared on my face because I couldn't wait to see her pretty pink pussy.

"Get out, Nate!" she hollered. KoKo tried to move around me, but I wouldn't allow it. She wasn't leaving until she heard everything I had to say to her.

"Why? So you can flaunt your ass for that nigga? How long you been cheating on me, KoKo?"

"Cheating on you? Are you being serious right now? I've never cheated on you a day in my life."

"Bullshit! There's no way we just broke up and you're already here with another man."

"At least I waited until we broke up to do it. That's more than I can say about you. Matter of fact, you wanna talk about something? Let's talk about the woman you had in our domain."

"Why you bringing up old shit?"

"Old shit? It's only been a month since that happened."

"Like I said, *old*! This is new. You here with him now," I barked. KoKo jumped as if she were startled by the deepness of my voice.

"I'm here with him now, but I'm not with you. Now move so I can leave!" she demanded.

"I thought you said you had to use the bathroom."

"I don't need help doing it. Either you're going to let me use it in peace, or you're going to let me out of here."

"What if I don't want to let you leave?"

"What's the problem, Nate? I wasn't good enough for you, because if I was, you wouldn't have had another trick in my house. I was good to you. Anything you wanted, you got. I didn't even make you work. You allowed me to go out here and do the job of a man while you freely did what you wanted." KoKo suddenly became teary-eyed.

"Don't start all that crying and shit. I don't want to hear it. That's the problem now. You did what you wanted to do. Now, bring your ass on back home."

"That is not my home. I've moved on, and I suggest you do the same."

"Don't play with me, KoKo."

"Who said I was playing? I'm serious as a heart attack. Now, get the hell out of my way. This is the last time I'm going to tell you to move."

KoKo was from the streets and popped a lot of shit, but I'd never known her to get into a fight. Even the incident with Michelle was a thing of luck. She wasn't the fighting type. She was the person that popped big shit, but that was all she did.

"And if I do—"

Before I could finish my statement, KoKo drew her foot back and allowed it to swing forward and kicked me dead between the legs. Grabbing my balls, I fell to my knees.

**Spifff...**

Within a matter of seconds, KoKo spit on me before yelling, "Next time I tell you to get the fuck out of my way... do it!"

KoKo left out the bathroom, leaving me rolling around on the floor with my hands over my balls. The strain could clearly be seen in my face as I struggled to regain feeling so I could stand.

"Oh my God... Are you okay?" someone came running into the bathroom to ask.

"I'm good. Just help me up," I told her.

The woman stood back and looked at me. She never said a word for at least two minutes before her hands finally flew up to her mouth.

"You tried to rape somebody," she hollered and ran out the bathroom.

At that point, I knew some shit was about to happen. She was going to go tell security, and that would mean I was done for. Doing the only thing I could think of, I got on all fours and crawled out of the bathroom. I went down the hall in the opposite direction of where the party was and tried to leave before anyone spotted me. Just my luck, the back door was locked, so there was no way out. I'd fucked up big time, and now the shit was about to come back to bite me.

## ❦ 15 ❦

## HASSAN (SAN)

"**B**aby, what's wrong?" I asked when KoKo came running back to me. She was frantic, so nothing she said made sense. I had to get her to sit down and take a drink in order to get her to calm down.

"He's in-in-in-in th-h-h-ee bath-ro-o-o-m..." she managed to get out in between breaths.

By that time, both Major and Kita were with us trying to figure out what was going on as well. There were so many people in the club that none of them paid attention to what was going on with us. Hell, it was my birthday, so you would've thought a nigga would've been getting more attention than he was. I already knew what the issue was. Major put everyone on high alert that I wasn't to be fucked with. He obviously didn't do too good of a job since a nigga wanted to try me and mess with my girl while we were at my party.

"Let's roll..." Major stated. We both touched our sides where we were strapped and ready for whatever.

Charging out of the VIP section toward the bathrooms, we found Nate's bitch ass balled up in a corner. If that fool was trying to hide, he did a piss-poor ass job.

"I'll take him to the basement. You get the girls out of here," Major stated.

"Naw. They don't need to know anything is up. Let's go handle his ass now, and we can deal with them later," I barked.

"You know the girls are going to come looking for us. We don't need them to know what the fuck we are about to do," he chided through clenched teeth. His jaws had tightened, which was a clear indication that he was ready to fuck some shit up.

*RATATATATAT... RATATATATATAT...*

Out of nowhere, shots rang out in the club. At that point, KoKo was the only person on my mind. Major and I knew we had to get back to the girls. Strategically, we covered each other as we made our way back over to our section. Bodies were dropping all around us. The shit was unreal. Somebody had fucked up big time gunning for us. Naw. That couldn't be the case. Nobody would be that fuckin' stupid.

When we stepped foot back inside the VIP, Kita was curled up under a table, but KoKo was nowhere to be found. We searched everywhere in the section for her.

"Where is KoKo?" I asked Kita. She was too panicked to speak. After a while, the shooting stopped. JT came rushing over to where we were to make sure we were good.

"Find KoKo," Major instructed him as we witnessed people hightailing it out of the club. They were knocking each other down and even stepping on one another. It was a horrific scene.

People were running around like chickens with their heads cut off. They didn't seem to know where they were going or how they were supposed to get there. We had to wait until the club was cleared out before we really had a chance to look for KoKo. JT rushed them out of the building so we could do a better search for her.

With everyone gone, we could hear sirens nearing the building. That wasn't a typical scene for us. We didn't even have a chance to get our story together before the cops came, and at that moment, I really didn't give a damn. Besides, it wasn't like we had done anything wrong. We were at a party, celebrating my life, and some idiots came in there shooting shit up for whatever reason. Hell, I wasn't even beefing with anybody, so I had no idea who would be dumb enough to do some shit like this. The only thought I really had was that this was some shit that didn't have anything to do with me.

"I can't find her any-damn-where," Major shouted when he came back to where I was standing.

"This doesn't make any sense. How could she just disappear like that?" Kita questioned.

"Do you think that nigga Nate could've grabbed her in the midst of all that shooting?" Major probed. That made a light bulb go off in my head. It had me wondering if he was behind the shooting. Could he have had someone on standby to shoot up the fuckin' club in the event that he didn't come out in a certain period of time? Could he have had someone kidnap KoKo? All kinds of thoughts ran through my mind, and they weren't good thoughts. Any bad thoughts that I had wasn't good for anybody.

"San?" Major yelled at me, bringing me back to the present.

"I'm not sure, but for his sake, that better not be the case. Find that nigga and bring him to me ASAP!" I ordered, banging my fist down on the table that was closest to me.

Nate's ass may have gotten away from us before, but that shit wasn't going to happen for a second time. I needed answers and his ass was going to be the one who had to give them to me.

## ❧ 16 ❧

## MARKITA (KITA)

W hen the guys went in search of Nate, I stayed back to make sure KoKo was going to be alright. She was doing a lot of crying because of whatever Nate had done to her. I couldn't wait for him to be out of her life for good. She deserved so much better than him. I was glad she was finally realizing that herself.

"I've got to get out of here," she told me as she grabbed the mini purse that she walked in with.

"You can't leave. We have to wait on the guys," I told her. She didn't want to hear what I had to say. She was determined to get as far away from Nate as she could, and I couldn't say that I blamed her.

"Fuck that. Call me later," she stated and proceeded to leave.

"Damn..." I exclaimed and went to gather my stuff too. There was no way I could allow her to leave by herself. Especially when we didn't know where Nate had gone or what the guys were doing.

The shots rang out as soon as I was about to follow KoKo out. Where she went from there, I didn't know. The only thing I could do was work to keep myself safe. KoKo was a smart woman, so I knew she'd get her ass out of dodge. That was the last time I saw her. Now, my nerves were all over the place worried about her. How the hell was I going to tell Tamir that I lost his mother?

"Here... She's over here!" I heard someone yell out. We were

95

still in the club searching everywhere to find her. Major and San had called in a whole slew of people and were giving out direct orders on what they wanted to happen. Seeing Major take charge did something to me. I was turned on and fascinated all at the same time.

"Where?" San hollered.

"Behind the bar," the man replied. We all took off running toward the bar as the man picked KoKo up and laid her on the bar. She was covered in blood and wasn't moving. My heart sank. I blamed Nate for all of this shit. Had he not showed up, then the boys wouldn't have gone to look for him, KoKo wouldn't have been trying to get away, and the guys would've been there to protect us.

"Who did this to her?" I cried as I placed my head on her chest. I just knew she was dead.

"Call 9-1-1!" San yelled, feeling all over KoKo. I was sure that was so he'd be able to check for a pulse.

"They are already en route. They were called when the shooting started," JT stated.

"Is she alive? Please tell me she's going to be okay. She has a son. She can't be dead. I need her," I continued to cry. My dress was soaked, but I didn't care. All I wanted was for my friend, my sister, to be okay.

"Come on, baby. Let me get you out of here," Major said. He came over and wrapped his arms around me. He tried pulling me away, but I started fighting him. There was no way I could leave KoKo. She needed me. She had no one else.

"Make room for the paramedics," JT hollered. Major picked me up and moved me out of the way. San stuck as close to KoKo as he could. He even rode to the hospital in the ambulance with her. The police started trying to question everyone else who remained at the scene, but no one would talk. How could we? We didn't know anything other than the fact that we were in there having a good time one minute, and the next minute, someone was shooting the club up, literally.

"Where is my purse? I need my keys," I announced.

"Come on. I'll take you," Major stated. He grabbed my hand and led me out the door. We got inside of his car, he turned the emergency flashers on, and we stayed on the bumper of the ambulance the whole time we traveled to the hospital.

Fidgety. Nervous. Frantic. There were so many words that could describe the way that I felt at that time. We made it to the hospital in no time. Major let me out in the front of the emergency room entrance while he went to park the car. I ran on the inside to the receptionist's desk. I was told that I would have to wait for the doctor to come out and talk to me.

Hassan and Major eventually joined me in the waiting room. They huddled up in a corner to themselves and were very secretly talking with one another. Being that I knew the line of work they were in, I could only imagine what they were talking about.

Pacing back and forth, it seemed like we'd been in the waiting area for days waiting to hear something about KoKo. It was driving me insane not knowing anything. I thought back to my parents and all the things they tried to instill in me and did the only thing I could think of doing at that moment. Dropping down to my knees, I placed my hands together on my mouth, closed my eyes, and began praying. God was the only one that could bring us out of this situation.

Feeling someone touch me on the shoulder, my eyes quickly opened. When I looked up, both Major and San had dropped down to their knees as well on both sides of me. They placed a hand on each of my shoulders and closed their eyes as well.

"Dear God, I know it's been a while since I've come to you, but I need you now more than ever. It's not for me, but it's for my best friend. She's a good woman. She didn't deserve to be shot. She has a great life ahead of her and a son that needs her. She's all he has. Please help her to pull through. I don't know what the hell else to say. Nate was on some fuck shit. He should be here, not her. That bitch ass ni—"

"Oh Lord, Our Heavenly Father..." Major cut me off and began saying a prayer. I'm sure it was because I allowed my emotions to get the best of me and started hollering out all kinds of things that I shouldn't have. They had to have understood where I was coming from. My girl didn't deserve this shit.

"Banks family..." someone yelled out, stopping Major from praying. We all jumped up from the floor and walked over to the medical personnel that was wearing dark-green scrubs.

"Yes," I said to the staff.

"Dr. Woodall would like to speak with you. Please follow me," the man stated. He walked us down a long hallway into what appeared to be a smaller waiting room. It was unpleasantly cold. Major must've sensed that I was worried because he pulled me close to him and held me tightly. "He will be right with you," the man told us and walked away.

"I don't like this," I confessed to Major and San.

"Don't think the worse. Let's see what he has to say and go from there," San said.

"That's easier said than done," I retorted.

"I know, but we prayed about it and turned it over to God. You can't do that and question His actions. Allow Him to work," Major rebutted.

"Excuse me, are you the family for Ms. Banks?" an older man with salt-and-pepper hair popped inside the room and asked. He was tall and looked fine as hell to be a doctor. His metal-framed glasses set halfway down his nose as he reviewed the chart that was in front of him and then looked at us.

"Ms. Banks just came out of surgery, and I must tell you that this was a very hard surgery. She suffered two gunshot wounds."

"Two? Where? How?" I started firing off all types of questions to the doctor.

"Calm down, Kita. Damn! Let the man speak," San barked.

"You're going to let him talk to me like that?" I asked Major.

"Not now, Kita. We have to find out what's going on with KoKo," he cosigned San. I was pissed but couldn't do shit about it because he was right. They both were. Our main focus was KoKo right now.

"Continue, Doc."

"The first bullet was in her thigh. It went in on the left side and came out through the back. It tore a few muscles, but no main arteries or ligaments were compromised."

"Thank God," I sighed.

"What about the other bullet?" San asked.

"The other one was in her chest. It was a through and through as well, but since it was in her chest, that one was the most detrimental. There were a few bullet fragments that we had to work slowly to remove. However, we were able to get them all removed. That's not what's concerning to us though," he paused. "It seems that when Ms. Banks was shot, she hit her head on her fall to the ground. I'm not sure what she hit it on, but it was a hard hit. She has some swelling to her brain. We've placed her in a medically induced coma until we can get the swelling to go down some. These next few hours are the most detrimental. We are going to have to keep a very close eye on her for now," he explained.

"Do you know how long she will have to be in this coma?"

"No, I don't. The healing will be left up to how well her body heals. Pray."

"Can we stay with her?"

"She's going to be in ICU, so you can only be with her during visitation times."

"No, I'm not going to leave her. We don't know who did this and they could come back. There's no way that we can leave her alone," I cried. My heart was broken.

"Can I speak with you in private?" San asked the doctor.

They walked off to the side before San came back and said, "I have my own private doctor coming in to see about KoKo, and she will have 'round the clock surveillance."

"I want to stay with her. I'm not leaving her, San," I told him, and I meant that shit.

"That's fine. I'm going to work that out with the hospital administrator. Chill out for now, ma. We got this," he assured me. "Give me some time to get this handled. I need to make a few calls. Go home and get some rest, I'll stay here with KoKo. Pack a bag of shit you'll need for about a week, and we can go from there," he added.

"Come on, I'll take you home," Major told me.

"Thank you, San." I thanked him before giving him a big hug. He had eased a lot of my worry when he said he was going to get it worked out so I could stay with KoKo.

"No problem. Oh, I need you to go by her place and get some stuff for her son too. He's going to be up here too."

"Wait... He doesn't need to see her like that."

"You have any other ideas? He has no other family to stay with, and you know I'm not trusting him to go with his punk ass dad. It'll be good for him to be here to talk to her. It may help her heal faster. Didn't they say they can hear you talking to them or some shit? He may be exactly what helps her out of this." What he said made sense, and he was right. We really didn't have any other choice.

There was no way we were going to be able to see KoKo before we left, so I went ahead and left with Major. San said he was going to stay at the hospital until we got back. It helped to know that someone who cared about her was going to be there in case something happened.

# NATE

"What the fuck happened back there?" I asked my cousin, Deja.

"What the fuck you mean what happened? What the hell you think happened?" she yelled. She hated when she was questioned about anything, but she knew damn well that I couldn't let her slide for that shooting. Too many innocent people were hurt, and we could get caught up behind that. I wasn't trying to spend my life sitting behind bars because her ass was trigger happy.

"I told you to have my back, not kill any-damn-body," I fussed.

"Nigga, shut your weak ass up. That's your problem now. You always worried about the wrong thing. You asked me to help you get your bitch, and that's what I was trying to do. When she ran to where San's ass was and I didn't see you come out, I had to do something."

"So you shot up a fuckin' club?"

"You act like I did the shit alone. I called my crew and told them we needed to handle some shit. Hell, it worked out in both of our favors. You wanted to get your girl and I wanted to spook

San's ass. He needed to know that he had competition in these streets," she boasted.

"That's bullshit and you know it. You killed people, and we didn't get KoKo. This was an epic fail," I barked.

"Mannnn... Fuck that bitch! If she don't want you, then leave her where she is. That bitch for everybody!" Deja hollered, which only infuriated me more.

Storming out of her house, I hopped in my car. I had to find KoKo to make sure she was okay. I didn't know where she lived, but I knew where Kita lived, so that was my first destination. Knowing I couldn't knock on her door, I sat in my car and waited for any sign that she was home. Her car wasn't there yet, so I figured there was a chance that she wasn't coming home tonight.

R&B softly flowed through my speakers as I laid my head back on my seat. I smiled reminiscing on the day that I met KoKo.

*KoKo was standing in front of the Jasco gas station in South Jackson with four of her friends. I'd just pulled up to get some gas and grab some smokes for my mother. We locked eyes, and I could immediately feel a connection with her. She was wearing these tight ass skinny jeans with some knee-high boots and a long-sleeved crop top. I'd always wanted to ask her why she was dressed like that when it was hot as hell outside, but I never did because I figured she was just hot in the ass. That made me want her even more. I could tell she was young by the way she was acting with her friends, but I didn't let that stop me from talking to her.*

*"Sup?" I said to all of the girls that stood with her. It was five of them, but she was the only one I was checking for.*

*"Hey," they all dryly spoke. KoKo never took her eyes off me.*

*"What's your name?" I asked her.*

*"KoKo. Yours?"*

*"When you put it in your phone, save it as your man. That's all you need to know." She giggled.*

*"Who said you were my man?"*

*"I'm telling you I am. You're wifey,"* I gassed her ass up. She blushed, showing her innocence. *This is going to be easier than I thought, I thought to myself and it was.*

A five-minute conversation turned into a four-year relationship. We had our ups and downs like any other couple, but I couldn't lie, KoKo was good to me. Shit, she was *too* good to me. Truth be told, I'd always thought she was too good to be with me. That was probably why I didn't try to do better for myself. If I held her down, then she'd never be able to leave me. That was something I always thought about. Nobody could've ever paid me to believe that thinking like that would backfire on my ass. Now, I was out here, looking stupid as fuck, wondering where she was and if I'd ever be able to get her back.

Finding myself dozing off, my eyes flew open when some headlights came zooming toward me. I watched as Kita got out of a car and ran inside of her house. She came back out probably thirty minutes later carrying a duffel bag. She hopped back in the car, and they went flying out of her driveway. I cranked up my car and began to follow them. They ended up outside of some townhouses that I wasn't familiar with. I noticed Kita getting out of the car and going inside of one. Whomever was driving her around pulled away. That was when I surveyed the parking lot and spotted KoKo's car outside.

Grabbing my gun from under the front seat, I hopped out the car. Observing my surroundings, I made sure nobody was watching before I went to the exact same townhouse that I saw Kita enter. I placed my ear up to the door to see if I could hear anything. When I didn't, I figured nobody was inside that I needed to worry about. Right when I was about to knock, I heard the doorknob twisting. Lucky for me, the townhouse she was in was on a corner, so it didn't take much effort for me to hide around the corner. Some strange woman that I'd never seen before came prancing outside. I watched as she got in her car and drove away.

Making my way back toward the front of the townhouse, I twisted the doorknob and was happy as hell to see that it wasn't locked. Pushing it open, I slowly made my way inside. With my gun unlocked and ready to use, I gradually made my way through each room.

Peeking through one of the doors, I was able to see Kita placing some stuff in a bag. From the looks of the way things were set up and the pictures on the wall, I knew that I was inside of KoKo's townhouse, but there was no sign of KoKo or my son anywhere.

"Where is she?" I asked, pushing the door open to the room that Kita was in.

"What the fuck? How did you get in here?" She jumped. She looked around the room and went to reach for the lamp, but I pointed the gun at her.

"I wouldn't do that if I were you," I advised her.

"Well, it's a good thing you aren't me," she told me and went for the lamp.

***Pow...***

Aiming the gun in the air, I sent a bullet flying. That was stupid as hell on my part because I knew someone would eventually call the police.

"So you're going to shoot me now? First KoKo and now me? Damn, you're ruthless as fuck, Nate."

"What do you mean about first, KoKo?"

"Oh, come on, Nate. Don't act like you don't know what happened."

"I don't know. What happened to KoKo?"

"So you're going to look me in the face and tell me that you were in the club when all those shots rang out and you don't know anything about KoKo being shot?"

"Yes, I'm going to tell you that because I didn't know that shit. Is she okay? Where is she? Where is my son? Huh? Where are they, Kita?" I questioned her, wondering where my family was.

"She's in the hospital fighting for her life, and you're here trying to take the life of her best friend. Do you think this is going to be the way for you to get her back? It's not! She doesn't want you, Nate. You hurt her for the last time. Why don't you see that?"

"Where is Tamir? Where is my son?" I asked her once more. I'd have to worry about KoKo later. With her being in the hospital, there was no way I'd be able to get to her. However, my son was another subject.

"He's not here," she stated, but I knew she was lying because she couldn't look me in the eyes. She was trying to hide something, but that wasn't going to work.

"Fuck it!" I got up on her and hit her in the head with the butt of the gun. She immediately dropped down to the floor. Running out of the room, I had to find my son. I began to open the doors to the rooms I hadn't already checked. The first door I opened was to the bathroom. The second door I opened was to a hall closet. It wasn't until I reached the third room that I located Tamir peacefully sleeping in his *Cars* bed.

Knowing it was only a matter of time before the cops or the person that dropped Kita off showed up, I went back inside of KoKo's room and grabbed the bag that Kita was placing shit inside of. I dumped all of its contents out and went back in the room with Tamir. I placed as many of his clothes and shoes inside of it that I could. I went inside the bathroom and grabbed all of his lotions, soaps, and other hygiene items. He had eczema, so he could only use certain things on his skin. Because I didn't have much money, I grabbed as much of it as I could get from KoKo's. Taking the bag out to the car, I went back inside the house and grabbed Tamir.

"Daddy?" he groggily asked as he wiped his sleepy eyes.

"Yes. Daddy got you, son," I told him and wrapped him in a blanket. Taking him out of the townhome, I placed him in the back seat of my car and strapped the seat belt over him.

Hopping back in the front seat, I noticed headlights coming

toward me once more. I waited until the car pulled in front of KoKo's townhouse and the driver got out. That was when I noticed it was Major's ass. I had to get the fuck out of dodge and fast. When he walked inside the house, that was when I cranked up and sped down the road. It was about to be a long and trying time, but I had my son where he needed to be. With me.

## ❧ 18 ❧

## MAJOR

Kita told me to drop her off at KoKo's so she'd be able to pack some things for KoKo and her son. I was hesitant about it at first, but I knew I needed to get gas and call my mother. That was the only reason I agreed. On my way back to pick her up, I'd called her several times to give her a heads-up that I was on my way back. When she didn't answer the phone, my nerves got the best of me. That was when I sped back down the road to get to where she was. Imagine my surprise when I made it back and found the door wide open. That wasn't smart at all, and I was prepared to go off on her about it until I found her knocked out in the back room.

"Kita? Baby, get up!" I kneeled down beside her and pleaded with her to get up. I was scared as hell and pissed at myself at the same time. How could I have not trusted my first mind and stayed with her? After all of the shit that happened at the club earlier, I knew it wasn't safe to leave her there alone, but I allowed her to talk me into it. That was possibly the worst mistake I ever could've made in my life.

"Major?" Kita said my name as she started to come to.

"I'm here, baby. Let me help you up," I insisted. That was when I picked her up and carried her over to the bed.

While Kita started to gather herself, I took my phone out and hit San up. I let him know that some shit had gone down, and he needed to get to KoKo's house ASAP. He reminded me that he was at the hospital and couldn't leave until we got back there. I told him that I'd key him in on what happened after I found out more.

"Baby? Are you okay? Can you tell me what happened?" I refocused my attention back on Kita once I'd ended my call with San.

"Nate." As soon as I heard his name, I wanted him dead. I regretted that I hadn't done it when I had the chance to do it earlier.

"What did he do to you?" I asked. My teeth clenched together, and my jawbone tightened. The more I thought about what I wanted to do to him, the more my blood began boiling.

"I'm not sure how he got in here, but when I was in here trying to pack some things up for KoKo, he came busting in the room, asking me where she was and where Tamir was. I confronted him about shooting her, but he acted like he didn't know anything about her being shot. The sad part is that, for some reason, I believe him."

"What? How could you believe a con artist like him? That nigga probably lies for a living," I asserted.

"I know, but I don't think that he was lying about that. He would've acted differently. That doesn't matter. His ass hit me in the head with a gun."

"What the fuck did you just say?"

"He was asking me about Tamir, and I tried to tell him that he wasn't here. I even attempted to hit him with a lamp. He shot in the air to stop me. In the midst of that, he must've realized I was lying about Tamir being here, and he hit me in the head with the gun to knock me out…" She paused. "Oh my God… Where's Tamir?" she cried before trying to get up off the bed.

"You stay here. I'll go look." I didn't want her getting up too fast, because I was worried that she would fall and hurt herself.

She'd just suffered blunt force trauma to the head, so I needed her to stay calm and relax as much as possible.

Handing her one of the guns that I carried with me, I told her to use it if she needed to. There was no way I was going to leave her unprotected again. Leaving her in the room, I searched the apartment to see if I could find Tamir. There was no sign of him anywhere. However, I did notice that the drawers were open and most of them were empty. Nate had taken Tamir and had no intentions of returning him.

"Kita, I need you to stay calm." I should've known better than to say that to her. As soon as the words left my mouth, she began crying harder. I sat next to her on the bed, and she placed her head in my lap. There was nothing I could say or do to change what happened.

"Why is this happening?" she continued to cry.

"Baby, I don't know. But I promise we are going to get him back. We are going to catch Nate's ass," I assured her. "Come on. We have to get out of here before the police show up. If they do, then we're going to have to tell them what happened, and we won't be able to handle him the way that we need to," I told her.

It took some time, but I was finally able to get her out of the house and into the car. I hit San up on my way back up to the hospital to let him know that something else had happened that we needed to handle ASAP. He told me I knew where he was, and he was right about that. Now, I had to figure out how I was going to tell him what happened. He and KoKo weren't together when he met Tamir, but I knew that he loved him. If anything were to happen to him, San was going to tear the whole mufuckin' city up, and that wasn't going to be good for anybody.

"Baby?" I said to Kita once I'd ended the call.

"Yeah?" she spoke just above a whisper.

"You know how San feels about Tamir. You're going to have to let me tell him what happened. Please," I pleaded with her because I knew how she was. She would act on emotion and tell him shit at the wrong time and when we were in the wrong place. She'd fuck around and have him shut the whole damn hospital down. "Please?" I asked again.

"Okay, baby," she softly replied.

"Thank you," I told her as I tried to get my mind right.

No matter what I said to San or how I said it, the shit wasn't going to be easy. Somebody was going to get hurt, and I could only hope it ended up being the right person.

# 19

# HASSAN (SAN)

There was not too much more that I'd be able to take. How the fuck could my twenty-fifth birthday turn out to be the birthday from hell? Shit, I was the boss in the streets, and right now, the only thing I felt was hopeless. The way shit happened tonight was careless as hell. That wasn't the type of move that a damn boss made. I was embarrassed as hell and knew that I was going to have to do something to redeem myself and my name.

Major called me twice to let me know something else had happened. There wasn't shit more I could take. The way he was talking let me know that it was going to be something to make me want to fuck some shit up and that wasn't going to be good for anybody.

Standing on the opposite side of the door, I looked in the glass door to see them placing all of these tubes and machines on KoKo. I'd never seen anyone like that in my life. Not in this state. It scared me because it looked as if she were dead, and that was something I never wanted to imagine.

Death was not something that hit close to home for me. All of the people that ran in my crew had been healthy and strong while working with me. There had been some that were killed or died after dealing with me but none while working for me. Like I said earlier, nobody had ever been crazy enough to come for me, so the shooting at the club really threw me for a loop.

"A couple of the cops that we have on payroll have decided to take some shifts on staying with KoKo," JT came over to me and said.

"That's cool. I was able to get the administrator on the phone so I could get everything set up the way that I needed. Make sure that everyone that enters the room with KoKo is fully covered in the PPE that I'm having brought in," I told him.

"Yeah, because Dr. Whitfield is en route here. He already has permission to work in the hospital, so he will be able to take care of KoKo's medical needs," he reminded me.

"I know. I already talked to the chairman of the board. I need them to rush the process to give him access, or I was going to have KoKo moved," I told him.

"That's what's up, man. You know Major on his way up here with Kita, right?"

"Yeah, he called me. He told me that some more shit went down. Do you know what happened?"

"Naw. I haven't spoken to them since they left. If anything, he would tell you what was going on before he said anything to me," he asserted, and he was right.

We both stood there watching as the medical staff got everything together that KoKo was going to need. I wasn't sure if she had insurance or not, but I wasn't too worried about it, because I knew I had more than enough money to cover all of her medical bills and still be able to live comfortably.

**Ring... Ring... Ring...**

Glimpsing down at my phone, I realized that it was Major calling me.

"I'll be right back. Don't let her out of your sight," I told JT.

"Bet," he replied, and I walked toward the waiting room while answering the phone. I needed to be as far away from other people as possible because I didn't know what Major was about to tell me.

"Yo?" I answered. "Where you at?"

"I'm waiting for you down by the cafeteria," he told me. Suddenly, a cold draft hit me. Something told me what he was about to tell me was going to add more to the anger I was already feeling.

Not rushing to find out anything else bad, I took my time walking the halls of the hospital. There was sadness all around me. I hated that shit. If I didn't dread being anywhere else in life, being in this hospital was definitely something I wasn't feeling. Had I been here for any other reason, I was sure things would've been different.

By the time I made it down to the cafeteria, Major was blowing my phone up again.

"Yo?" I answered, letting him know that I was frustrated.

"Where you at?"

"I just made it down here. What the fuck is so important that you couldn't go ahead and tell me over the phone?" I sneered.

"We got a big ass problem, San," he loudly spoke. Out of nowhere, I felt someone touch me. I turned around with my fists up ready to pounce on whomever it was until I saw that it was Major.

"Damn. Chill your scary ass out. It's just me," he said with a smirk on his face.

"Nigga, fuck you! Nobody wasn't no damn scared. If anything, you should've been scared of what I was about to do to your ass," I muttered. "Now, what the fuck is up?"

"We got a problem," Major stated.

"You don't think I know that? If we didn't, we wouldn't be down here. Tell me what it is and quit beating around the bush." I knew it had to be something bad because of the way that Major was acting.

Major and I were first cousins. When I started coming up in this street game and needed somebody I could trust on my team, he was the first person I called. We grew up together, and I knew he didn't take any shit. If anything were to happen to me, I knew he'd be the first person to shut some shit down to get answers. I respected that. Plus, I never had to question his loyalty.

"I need you to remember where we are and try to stay calm when I tell you this."

"Would you spit it out already?"

"Tamir is missing," he finally said.

"Come again?" I asked him to repeat what he'd said. There was no way I heard him correctly.

"Tamir is missing. Kita and I went to go get him and some clothes for him and KoKo to bring up here. I went to go handle something, and while I was gone, Nate ran in on Kita, knocked her out, and took Tamir."

"If you trying to be funny, this ain't the time. Where my lil' guy at?" I probed.

KoKo hadn't been around me long, but the time I did spend with her, I also spent with Tamir. She wouldn't let him out of her sight. She always told me that she thought Nate would try to kidnap him, but I didn't think his ass was stupid enough to really do it.

"Where is he?" I asked Major. He knew me well enough to know that I didn't like information handed to me without substance. If Nate took Tamir, I needed answers on where he could've gone with him.

"I'm not sure, but we know that Nate has him."

Hearing Major tell me that Tamir was missing really fucked me up. He was pulled into an adult situation, and for what? I could never understand how a grown ass man could do his woman wrong and want to punish her for walking away from his ass. The shit was crazy and fucked up at the same time. KoKo was going to be livid when she heard this shit.

"How am I going to tell KoKo this?" I roared, flipping over tables and chairs that were near me. Hospital security started running toward us, but Major told them to stand back. When they saw how angry I was, they stopped in their tracks. Touching me was going to land their asses inside of one of those damn hospital beds.

"Calm down, San. You see where we are. They are going to ban you from this fuckin' hospital if you don't stop. Then who's going to be here taking care of KoKo?" At the sound of her name, I stopped. KoKo was really all that mattered right now. I had to get myself together to beat the streets to find Tamir.

"Get the crew together now! I want that nigga's head brought to me by the end of the night!" I roared. It was time for me to stop playing with Nate's ass. Had we gone ahead and killed him when we had his ass earlier, then none of this shit would be happening. It was fuckin' unreal.

Not only did I have to find the niggas that shot up my party. I also had to find Tamir and the nigga that was the cause of him being missing.

"I'm already on it. I got them combing the streets as we speak. I need to go check on Kita. That nigga hit her in the head with a gun, and I got them checking her out. Go back up there with KoKo, and I'll get everything handled," Major told me.

"Bet."

There was no reason for me to question Major because whenever he said he was going to take care of something, he did just that. I knew one thing for damn sure: I couldn't wait to wrap my hands around Nate's neck. That shit was bound to happen sooner rather than later.

# 20

## NAKITA (KITA)

Major had to persuade me to see the doctor when we got back to the hospital. Although I said that I was good, he wanted to make sure Nate didn't hit me hard enough to cause any bleeding or swelling around my brain. I didn't want to see anybody, because I wanted to get to Tamir, but I had no choice.. Major had men guarding the whole hospital. They were not going to let me get away easily.

When he left to go see San, I turned away from the emergency room and went to where KoKo was being privately kept. I knew that, if anything, San would've added me to the list to see her. I bumped into JT when I got up there.

"Hey, sis," he greeted me, giving me a hug. He held me a little too long, which caused me to feel a little uncomfortable, but I didn't say anything. I simply pulled back from him. "What the fuck happened to your head?" he asked, his voice raised high as hell.

"It's okay. I got hit, but I'm fine."

"Did Major do this shit? I told that clown about putting his hands on wo—" He paused in midsentence.

"What did you just say?" I wanted him to repeat what he said because there was no way I'd heard him correctly. Was he trying to tell me that Major beat women? *What the fuck*, I thought.

"You know how Major is," he commented.

"No, I don't know shit. Major has never put his hands on me or made me think that he hit women. He's always been so loving and caring around me," I explained.

"That nigga a wolf in sheep's clothing. You've never seen his dark side."

"And I don't plan on it." I interrupted him. "Look, we not about to do this. I'm not sure what's going on with you or why you think I should look out for Major, but I'm good."

"I just don't want to see anything happen to you. Watch your back at all times." JT was starting to scare me. What the fuck was he trying to imply?

"I need to see my friend. Is it cool?" I felt like a kindergartner asking their teacher for permission to go pee.

"Yeah, go ahead. Make sure you put on all of that PPE. San don't want nobody going in there unprotected and risk KoKo getting some type of infection or something."

"A'ight."

Doing what I was told, I was covered from head to toe in protective gear. The way San was looking out for KoKo was amazing. I prayed that Major would do the same if it were me in here.

"Hey, baby!" I greeted KoKo, even though I knew she wasn't able to speak back. "I hate seeing you like this. I would trade places with you in a heartbeat," I honestly told her. KoKo cared for everybody. She would give the shirt off her back, which was why it really hurt me to see her laid up like this. "KoKo, I need you to get better. This may sound selfish, but I need you. Tamir needs you. You're almost done with school. You've been able to show your parents and other people that have doubted you that, even with a baby, you can still achieve your hopes and dreams. I admire that about you. So what we shake a little ass? Let me rephrase that because we know you got more than a little ass," I stated and started laughing. KoKo and I would always mess with each other about whose ass was bigger. I used to say it was mine, but that girl had an ass big enough to sit a whole damn Big Mac meal on top of it.

Damn, I did my best to hold back the tears that were threatening to fall from my eyes. I hated seeing her like that. It had to have been the worst thing I ever experienced in my life. My girl didn't need to be laid up like this. If she had to be laid up anywhere, it needed to be on a beach watching her son play in the sand. The thought of her son made me want to tell her what was going on with him, but I couldn't. I couldn't tell her that her son came up missing on my watch, because something told me she'd never be able to forgive me. I was careless. We knew that Nate was crazy, but I never figured he was *that* crazy. Because of what he pulled on her at the club, I should've been more aware of my surroundings and never given him the benefit of the doubt.

After sitting there for a while and pondering over what I needed to do, I made up in my mind that I was going to be the one to find Nate. It was me that he took Tamir from, and it was going to be me that got Tamir back.

"I love you, KoKo. If I've never told you that before, I love you." Placing a kiss on her forehead, I stood from my seat and went to where JT was.

"Where you headed? That was a quick visit," he said.

"I know. I got to go see the doctor before Major gets mad at me." I noticed JT roll his eyes when I said Major's name, but I didn't address it, there was no need to. If he was on some snake shit, that would come out soon. I could feel it.

"A'ight. Be careful, baby girl," he said, trying to pull me in for another embrace, but I threw my hand up to stop him.

With the PPE still over my body, I took the stairs down to the basement. I was thankful that Major had left his keys with me. It was great that I was still covered because I looked like medical staff, so when I left out of the hospital, nobody tried to stop me. I ran toward the parking lot by the emergency room and hit the alarm button on Major's car. When it went off, I turned the alarm off, got inside, and sped away from the hospital. Nate's ass had to be found, and it had to be tonight. I'd deal with Major's ass later.

# ❦ 21 ❧

## MAJOR

S tanding in the cafeteria trying to calm San down, my phone
went off alerting me that the alarm on my car was going off.
I called down to Domo to tell him to go check to make sure my
car was good. I played about a lot of fuckin' things, but my car
wasn't one of those things. Domo called me and told me that my
car was gone. I was furious. Who the fuck was dumb enough to
steal my damn car? First, somebody shot at me. Now, they stole
my car. Not to mention Nate's dumb ass had the audacity to hit
my girl. Kita was another thing I didn't fuckin' play about. The
thought of Kita made me remember that I left my keys with her.
She was supposed to be seeing the fuckin' doctor, and her
mufuckin' ass done left the hospital. I pondered over how the
hell she was even able to leave because we were supposed to have
every entrance locked down in the event Nate tried to come in
here fuckin' with KoKo. That was when I decided to call her lil'
ass. She thought she was slick, but I was slicker.

"Hey, baby," she answered the phone, trying to play innocent.

"Hey, boo. What you doing?" I asked. I wanted to see if her
ass was going to tell me the truth or not.

"Seeing the doctor," she lied. That crushed me because I
never pegged her as one that would lie to me.

"Oh, what room you in? I'm going to come check on you."

"Huh?"

"Huh, hell! Where the fuck you at, Kita?"

"I'm around."

"Kita, don't mufuckin' play with me. You see shit is hot, and you out here playing games and shit. I got the alert that your ass had my alarm going off in my car. You better not wreck my shit."

"Oh, so you called because you were worried about your lil' car and not your woman? What kind of shit is that?" There her ass went trying to play a fuckin' victim. I hated when she did that shit. That was the norm for her whenever we would get into it. That was her way of trying to get me to conform to whatever she wanted.

"Don't play with me. You know damn well why I'm calling you. Where are you?"

"I'm sorry, but I had to go look for him. I went to go see KoKo, and she was laid up there looking all peaceful. I felt like my best friend was dead. I didn't want to add on to the things she was feelings, so I had to leave. I have to do what I can to bring Tamir back to her. It's my fault he's missing," she cried. The sadness could be heard all in her voice, and I hated that. My baby was a good woman, but she kept getting into some fucked-up situations.

"Baby, it's not your fault. You can't control what the fuck he did. Come back here and let me go with you. It's too dangerous for you to be out there by yourself," I advised her.

"Do you want a weak woman?" she asked, catching me off guard.

"Why would I want a weak woman?" I probed.

"Exactly! You don't want or need a weak bitch on your team. Let me do this, Major."

"This shit ain't about you being strong or weak but about you not being stupid and getting yourself killed. I'd never be able to live with myself if something happened to you. Please just come back and let me help you," I damn near begged. Kita's lil' ass was doing something to me, and I didn't like that. Her defiance was pissing me off though. I couldn't deal with a woman that was so damn disobedient.

"No, I can't. I got to do this alone. I need to prove to you and KoKo that I can fix anything that I mess up."

"Nobody's doubting you, Kita. Just get back here, please."

"Okay, fine." Kita hung up the phone without giving me the chance to say anything else. I wanted to stay on the phone with her until she made it back to me in case something happened. At least I would be able to know what happened and where she was when it happened. She just didn't see how dangerous all this shit was. It had me questioning if she was really ready for my lifestyle.

Don't get me wrong, there had been several plans made for me to walk away from the street shit. Just like many other men, I didn't want to be doing this shit for the rest of my life. At the same time, I knew that now wasn't the time for me to be walking away. San and I ran this shit with an iron fist. Mufuckas knew not to cross us. That shit that happened tonight had to be some outsiders or some nigga that really had a death wish. Either way, their ass was dead for the shit they pulled.

Standing outside, I waited around for Kita's ass to pull back up. The alert hadn't been too long coming through my phone, so I knew her ass couldn't have made it too far. As I waited for her, I went ahead and hit up the crew to let them know what needed to be done in order to find Nate and Tamir. We had to get that little boy back to KoKo because if something were to happen to him, I was sure KoKo wouldn't want to fuck with any of us anymore. Even if it wasn't our fault.

After thirty minutes of standing out there, I gave up. Her ass wasn't coming back. She made up in her mind that she was going to do what she wanted to do, no matter how dangerous I told her it was. So I made up my mind what I was going to do about our relationship. If she wanted to be on her independent shit, she was going to do it without me.

## 22

## NATE

"Mommy... I want Mommy..." Tamir cried for KoKo.

All Tamir did was hoot and holler about wanting to see KoKo's ugly ass. It had started to wear on me because I didn't like the fact that he was more worried about his mother than he was about me. I was the one he was always with day in and day out. So why the fuck would he push me to the side for a woman that was barely there for him?

"Mommy is gone to heaven," I told him. His eyes bucked, which amazed me because he acted as if he'd been here before. You would've thought he knew what I was talking about when I said that she was gone to heaven.

"Don't tell that baby that," my mother fussed at me before coming to scoop Tamir out of my arms.

My mother and I didn't have the best relationship, because I still dwelled on how she put me out when I wasn't able to support her drug habit. It had me thinking about all the times she chose drugs over me. That wasn't something I wanted my son to know about, so I decided to keep my mouth closed. The only reason I was around her was because KoKo didn't know that I talked to her from time to time. If she sent someone after me, this would be the last place they would look.

"What? I'm telling him the truth?"

"What truth? From what you told me, all you know is that she was shot, and I'm not even sure if you know if that was true or not. What exactly did Kita say to you?" my mother questioned me.

One thing I could say about my mother was that even though she didn't mess with a lot of people, she had a lot of respect for KoKo. She didn't know her and really didn't care for her, but she liked how she stepped up to the plate and made sure I was good. Something her ass should've been doing. Let her tell it, that was neither here nor there. In other words, it didn't matter that she was no good as a mother as long as her child was taken care of. Sad, right?

"Come on, boy. Tell me what she said?" my mother demanded.

"She said that they were involved in a shooting and KoKo was shot. She said something about her being in the hospital fighting for her life," I told her once more. I didn't tell her that I was there because she would be able to put two and two together.

"That's so stupid of you. You know you're facing a life sentence if that girl dies, don't you?" she fussed.

"Why would I be facing a life sentence? I'm not the one who shot her?" I ranted.

"Because, dummy, you recruited your unstable ass cousin to help you get KoKo back, and she was shot in the process. You think them white folks gonna care that all you were trying to do was get your family back together? Hell naw. They are going to dwell on the fact that you got somebody to help you corner somebody who was ultimately shot and died in the process. That's life, nigga!" she hollered. "Don't think I don't know what really happened."

My mother turned her head away from me. I already knew she did that because she was about to cry. That killed me about her. She was always so worried about people seeing her as weak that she would always hide her tears.

"Ma, I would never do anything to hurt KoKo. I love her," I admitted.

"That's funny considering the fact that she's laid up in the hospital fighting for survival and you done kidnapped her son," she sneered.

"What kinda shit is that? He's my son too. I didn't kidnap him. Why the hell does everybody think a child is supposed to be with their mother? Nobody wasn't thinking that shit when the bitch was shaking her ass on a pole for all these random ass men."

"She was doing that to provide for y'all. You sound real stupid right now."

"Whose side are you on? I'm your child, not her." She was making me angrier by the minute taking up for KoKo. Why couldn't anybody see things from my side?

"Son, listen to me. I know that he's your son too, but you have to be real with yourself. I'm not saying you don't love him, but you're using him as a pawn. You always have, and you always will."

"Pawn? Fuck is you talkin' 'bout?" I wanted her to explain her dumb ass reasoning for why she thought my son needed to be with his mother.

"I've listened to you talk ever since you and that girl broke up. I watched you come around with your son when y'all were together. You were here with him in body, but your mind was never on him. You were worried about that studio and chasing after these lil' hot pussy ass girls. You kept him because you had no choice. If you could've found another babysitter, you would've because your main concern has been running the streets. When you and that girl broke up, you wanted to keep him because you knew she'd either have to keep forking out money to make sure he was good, or she'd have to come back home to you. If you want me to be completely honest with you, you stopped loving her a long time ago. The only reason you stayed was because you had nowhere else to go and probably couldn't find another woman on this earth to take care of you the way that she was," my mother freely spoke. Everything she said was the truth. I wasn't saying that I didn't love my son, but if I had things my way, I'd have someone else to watch him so I could do the shit I wanted to do.

The girl being at our house wasn't a coincidence, and it wasn't the first time. I'd cheated on KoKo several times, but I'd never been careless enough to let her catch me more than a few times. I guess I'd given up hope on us and stopped caring. It was either that, or I had in my mind that she had too much to lose by walking away from me so even if she caught me, she wouldn't have left.

"Mommy... Mommyyyyyy..." Tamir cried. He even went as far as falling out on the floor, kicking and screaming.

"Tamir, get your ass up and go to the back room, now," I told him. He completely ignored everything I said and continued to throw his temper tantrum.

***Pop... Pop...***

Bending over, I popped him twice on his lil leg. That only made him scream a little louder.

"You know what you got to do," my mother snidely commented. I glimpsed up at her and saw the smirk on her face. Although I hated to do it, she was right. Tamir had gotten out of hand and that had to be corrected immediately.

Dreadfully, I slowly took my belt off. My mother was going to get too much humor out of me spanking Tamir, so I made up in my mind that I wasn't going to do it in front of her.

"Get up, Tamir," I yelled. The more he cried, the madder I got.

After telling him a few more times to get up, when he didn't do it, I yanked him up by his little arm and threw him over my shoulder. I carried him to the back room and slammed the door behind me.

Tamir didn't understand how much it was going to hurt me more than it was going to hurt him. I used to hate when my mother told me that as a parent, but I now understood what she meant. It broke my heart to hear him scream as I tossed him on the bed and whooped him. Each time the belt made contact with his body, he would scream louder. He even went as far as rolling on the floor.

**Bam... Bam... Bam...**

The beating on the door was the only thing that stopped me from whooping him. It was as if I blacked out because I started thinking about how angry I was at KoKo for giving up on us. Her ass could've tried to talk through this shit with me. Yeah, I cheated on her a lot of fuckin' times, but she only caught me that one time. Every other time she found out about it was because the silly bitches I fucked with told her. She never had any real proof, so she stayed. But this last time was too much for her. Technically, she didn't even really catch me, because she made it home before the girl and I could get things poppin'. Why couldn't she be like most other women and forgive and move on? She was ready to jet the door after that one time and my dick hadn't even gotten wet. I refused to let her leave me, and I didn't even get to test drive the pussy.

**Bam... Bam... Bam...**

"What?" I snatched the door open. My mother was standing on the other side of it profusely sweating.

"What's your problem?"

"Do you not hear that he is no longer crying?" she asked me.

That was when I looked down and noticed that Tamir was laying on the floor curled up in the fetal position. I was scared as fuck. What had I done?

"We've got to get him to the hospital," she told me as she rushed to his side.

"No. He's fine. Leave him alone," I barked.

"Hell no. He could die. Something is wrong," she cried.

"Move, Momma. He's my son. He's okay," I tried my best to

assure her, but I didn't know my damn self if he was fine or not. I was scared.

"Boy, get your dumb ass out the way. I'm calling the fuckin' ambulance," she snapped as she pushed past me, I was sure to go searching for her phone.

While she was gone, I wrapped Tamir up in a blanket and rushed to the car. Cranking it up, I zoomed out of the driveway with nowhere in particular in mind. There was no way I could take him to the hospital. The police would arrest me for sure. That was when I made up in my mind what I would do.

Pulling up at the J-TRAN station, which was attached to the bus station, I made sure to park out of view of a camera so my car wouldn't be seen. Putting on my oversized hoodie, I scooped Tamir up and walked toward the station. When I reached the first bench, I laid him down, placed a kiss on his forehead, and hightailed it back to my car.

Throwing the car in drive, I jetted away from the station. I prayed that everything would be okay with my son. Somebody was going to find him. They had to. I just hoped it was in enough time to save him. I couldn't be saved, but he could.

## ❧ 23 ❧

## GERALDINE

Nate left the house, trying to hide what he'd done, but there was no way I could let that happen. Tamir was a good little boy and didn't deserve what happened to him. When Nate left the house, I rushed back to the bedroom to check on Tamir. Noticing that he was nowhere to be found, I searched the entire house, only to come up empty-handed again. That meant Nate had taken him. I'd already gotten ready for bed, but I didn't have time to change, so I had to slide my house shoes on and run on out the door. Housecoat, rollers, and all. Thankfully, there was only one way on and off my street, and I lived all the way on the end, so I knew which direction Nate had gone in.

Jumping in my car, I rushed down the road in search of them. I neared the back of two cars, and neither of them were him, so I drove around them. When I came upon a third car, it was driving slow as hell. I knew it wasn't Nate, because he was manic at this point. He wasn't going to be driving too slow trying to find a way to hide what he'd done.

*Beeeeppppppppp...*

I blew the horn, hoping whomever it was would get out of my way. I even went as far as turning on my emergency flashers. When that didn't work, I got beside them and let my window down. It was Kita's ass. What the hell was she doing by my house? Waving my hand, I flagged for her to let her window down.

"What are you doing?" I asked once she'd let it down.

"I'm looking for your son," she stated.

"How did you know where I lived?" I queried. As far as I knew, KoKo didn't even know Nate was dealing with me like that.

"KoKo told me. We've known for a while. She just never said anything because she wanted Nate to have a relationship with you." That touched me and angered me at the same time. It touched me because I thought she didn't want my son to have anything to do with me. That was all he used to tell me whenever he would come around and not bring her. It had me thinking she thought she was too good to be around me and she didn't want my grandson around. It angered me because Nate had me hating that girl for nothing. That was a shame. She was the one taking care of him, and he was throwing her under the bus to make himself look good. I guess he figured the truth would never come out as long as he kept her away from me.

*Beeeeppppppppp...*

Kita blew the horn at me to get my attention. Glimpsing up, I noticed a car coming right toward me. I hit my brakes so Kita could move up some and I could jump behind her. Once the car had passed, I moved back around to the side of Kita.

"Nate has Tamir," I hollered to her. Was it wrong of me to tell on my son? Not at this point because he had my grandson, and I knew that he wasn't mentally stable. Nate was gone, but there was still hope for Tamir. I'd never be able to forgive myself if something serious were to happen to him on my watch.

"I know. He took him from me. We have to find him," she informed me. That was when I looked up and saw the bruise over Kita's eye. Nate had put in some work on her head. It was sad. My son wasn't raised like that.

Being a young mother was the worst thing that could've ever

happened to me. I wasn't ready to raise anybody's baby when I was a baby myself. That was why I'd gotten rid of the first three or four babies I had before Nate. The only reason I kept Nate was because I'd been searching for something in men that I could never find... love. Then someone told me that if I wanted to have unconditional love, I needed to lean on my child. So my dumb ass had Nate, and he had been nothing but a headache ever since he came out of my pussy. When he got old enough to start hustling, I made him hit the streets to take care of me. It was nice having someone doing the things for me that I always wanted. Then he started wanting to do that rap shit and fucked everything up. Money that should've come to me went to the studio. That made me despise him. That nigga couldn't rap to save his life. If he just wanted to rap so bad, he needed to find a job wrapping Christmas gifts because that nigga was awful. I couldn't tell him that, because then he'd say I wasn't supporting his dream, and he probably would've stopped taking care of me. It was just a mess.

"Where did he go?" Kita yelled out.

"He went that way," I pointed to the end of the long street we were on.

"You go that way, and I'll go that way," she directed. When you reached the end of the street, you had to turn either left or right. She was going to the left, and I was going to the right.

Before we split, I hollered out my number and told her to call me if she found him. She put my number in her phone and quickly called me so I'd have hers before we turned off.

It seemed like I'd been driving for hours. I'd given up hope after the first thirty minutes of not being able to find him. I stopped at a light on Capitol Street thinking I should just turn around and go home. Right when I was about to call Kita to tell her I didn't have any luck, I looked around once more. That was when Nate's ass came zooming past me on Gallatin Street. Quickly, I jumped behind him. I wasn't worried about following too closely because I knew once his paranoia set in, he would be too worried about what his next step was going to be to notice anybody following him. Calling Kita, I told her where I was, and she needed to get to me immediately.

Nate began to slow down as we got near the bus station that was connected to the J-TRAN station. J-TRAN was the public transportations system in Jackson. Nate suddenly stopped, causing me to slow down. I turned my lights off to not alert him that someone could see him. He parked away from the building, and I was sure it was because he didn't want the cameras to see him. If he noticed me, then he'd run again, so turning off the lights was the best option.

Nate exited his car and studied the area for a minute. I was sure he was looking to see if anyone could see him. When he didn't see anything, he popped the trunk. I could've fainted when I saw him pull the blanket out the back. I already knew what it was. My heart fell to my feet and my nerves got the best of me. I wanted to jump out of the car and run to him, but I couldn't. He'd probably throw my grandbaby back in that trunk, and I'd never see him again. That was when I reached for my phone and called Kita again.

"Kita, where are you?"

"I'm on Gallatin. What direction did you go in?"

"We are parked near the bus station, but don't pull in until I tell you to," I told her.

"Why? He's going to get away!" she screamed.

"Bi—" I had to catch myself. I hated when hoes hollered at me, especially them young ones. "Girl, shut up and listen. I have eyes on him. I'm watching his every move. He's not going to get away. Don't hang up this phone," I directed her. I told her that because I wanted to give her play by play of what he was doing, and I needed her to jump into action when I told her to.

My eyes stayed on Nate the entire time he moved, and I would tell Kita everything I was seeing. I told her to turn her lights off if she could and get as close to the station as possible as I continued to tell her what was going on. I watched as my son placed Tamir on a bench like he was a dead dog and take off running as if it was nothing. Out of nowhere, Kita turned her lights on and whipped her car right in front of that bench. Nate's ass kept running. He didn't stop to look back. I followed behind his ass because there was no way I was going to let him get away.

Silently, I prayed that Tamir was okay. He didn't deserve that shit. I never should've suggested to Nate that he whooped him in the first place. Nate was unstable, and that was no secret. Never in a million years would that had been something I suspected because I'd never seen him so out of it before. Was he so hurt about KoKo leaving him that it had to come to this? Or was it that he didn't like the fact that he was no longer in control of what was happening in his life?

Nate drove all the way to Hattiesburg, MS. That was only an hour and a half away, but it was late, and I was tired. That didn't matter because I stayed right behind his ass. He must've gotten tired too because I noticed him pull into a hotel off Highway 49. He pulled right up in front of it and went inside.

**_Ring... Ring... Ring..._**

"Hello," I answered when I saw that it was Kita. "Is he okay?" I asked.

"Yeah, he's fine actually," she told me.

"Huh? How could this be?"

"He has one little mark on him and that's it. But I have him at the hospital getting him checked out," she stated.

Suddenly, I replayed everything that happened that night in my head. When I beat on the door and had Nate open it, I was shocked at the scene before me. Nate was exhausted and Tamir was on the floor in the fetal position. It had me wondering what really happened in that room. Had Nate blacked out and didn't know what really happened? Tamir must've fallen on the floor and Nate didn't notice. That meant that Tamir had possibly fallen asleep on the floor.

"Where are you?" Kita asked me.

"Why? Tamir is fine. There is no reason to get the police involved," I informed her.

"Police? Who said something about the police?"

The moment she said that, I already knew she was about to send those goons after my son. I despised the shit he did and how he changed my life, but I didn't want to see him dead. Now, if something were to have happened to Tamir, that probably would've been a different story because that would've been my fault. My son's death was not about to be on my hands over a mistake.

"Geraldine, tell me where you are. I just want to talk to Nate to tell him how he hurt me," Kita lied her ass off.

"Kita, I'm old, not dumb. I know exactly what you are trying to do, and that's not going to happen. Good fuckin' night," I hollered into the phone and hung up.

With Tamir being fine and knowing that Nate was safe, my job was done. I didn't have the money to get a hotel room, so I moved my car to the back of the parking lot. I parked between two big trucks and let my seat back. My phone was sitting right next to me, so I pulled it out and opened my clock app. I set my alarm for 10:30 since I knew check out time for most hotels were at eleven. To me, 10:30 would be enough time for me to get a little sleep and wake up before everybody started to leave. That way, I wouldn't get caught. I took my robe off and placed it over me to help knock some of the chill I was feeling off.

***Knock... Knock... Knock...***

It seemed like the minute my eyelids closed, someone knocked on my window. I jumped up startled because nobody there knew me. When I locked eyes with Nate, I damn near pissed myself.

"Let the window down, Momma," he ordered, motioning his finger for me to follow his directions.

Hesitantly, I let the window down.

"Why are you here?"

"I was scared. Where is Tamir?" I already knew the answer to that, but he didn't know it. At least I didn't think he did.

"Don't play dumb. I know you followed me. I also saw Kita when she came flying up when I left Tamir on that bench. You working with the enemy now? How do you even know her?"

"I saw her when I was coming to look for you. I knew her because of all the pictures you showed me of KoKo and her together. Remember you used to tell me how she spent more time with her friend than you and you thought that they may have been bumping cats or some shit," I ranted. I was saying any and everything I could to get out of whatever he might try to do to me.

"You didn't answer my question... You working with the enemy now?"

"No, I was worried. I didn't want anything to happen to Tamir."

"I'm your son, and you worried about the next lil' nigga."

"What the fuck did you just say? That's your son, my grandson."

"Was!" he hollered, pounding his fist on the top of my car. I jumped, seeing how enraged he was. Had I fucked up?

"Baby, I'm sorry. You could've gone to jail for murder. I didn't want that for you. I don't want any of this for you," I honestly told him because that was the truth. I hated that he was going through all the things that he was going through. It was horrific, and I couldn't imagine how he was feeling at this given moment.

"You don't give a damn about anybody but yourself. Let's be real, the only reason you came was because you thought if something happened to Tamir, you would've gone to jail too. You were worried about yourself and not anybody else," he chided, and he was right. There was really nothing I could say because there wasn't shit left to be said. Then I thought about what he said. He said *if* something happened to Tamir.

"Wait... So you knew Tamir was fine?" I quizzed.

"Yes, I knew. I knew that keeping him wasn't in my best

interest either. I saw him when he got on the floor, and I kept hitting the bed to make you think I was beating him. I'm not an animal. I could never harm my child. Despite what you or anyone else may think of me, I love Tamir, and I was a damn good father. Yeah, I left him with you a lot of times, but that didn't mean shit. You don't know half the shit I did with him when we were at home or that I took him to the park often or out to play with other little kids. That's what you get for judging a book by its cover. Next time go off facts," he muttered. That made me feel worse than I already did, and he had me looking stupid. That was that bullshit right there, but it was my fault because he was right. "Here," he said, handing me a key to the hotel.

"I saw you following me, and I know you're tired. Here's the key to a room. You're in room 204. Get some sleep and take your ass home," he said and began to walk away. He made it approximately five feet before he turned around and said, "Oh, and Momma..."

"Yes?" I cheerfully answered, thinking there was a chance he was going to give me some money or even tell me that he loved me. I was fuckin' wrong.

"This time when I tell you to stay the fuck away from me, I mean that shit. Don't come near me. I don't want shit else to do with you for as long as I have air in my body. I'm going to get my family back, and you won't be a part of it," he snarled and walked away. He didn't even give me a chance to explain myself or express how I was feeling. I guess he said that my ass didn't matter at this point. He was finally making his life about him. While I could be mad at him, I really couldn't. He had to focus on him. That was the same thing I should've done years ago. Damn, I should've swallowed his ass.

## ✣ 24 ✣

## NAKITA (KITA)

It was shocking to me that Nate's mother would work with me to help find Tamir. However, I was glad that she did. It was clear to me that Nate had been feeding her lies about KoKo by the expression on her face when I told her that KoKo knew about Nate making contact with her. What reason would KoKo have for Nate to not talk to his mother? Hell, she really hoped he would get to a point where he would move in with her, but that never happened.

Truth be told, KoKo loved Nate, but she was no longer happy with him. She was tired of working her ass off and trying to better herself and all he did was sit around the house and do nothing. She appreciated the fact that he looked after Tamir because he was so young and she didn't want to put him in a daycare yet. Besides, she worked at night, so there was no way she would be able to find somebody else to keep him. If her parents would've done right by her, she would've at least been able to get them to watch him. But that wasn't the way things went. We all knew things barely go the way we want them to go.

As soon as I spotted Nate, I couldn't wait. I had to get to him to find out where Tamir was. When I saw him lay something out on the bench, I knew exactly what it was. It fucked me up that a man could do his own child that way. I placed my hand on the gun I still had from Major and was ready to use it on Nate. Hell, he didn't give a damn when he hit me with one, so why should I care if I shot his ass with one?

Swooping in front of the train station, I hopped out and ran towards the bench. Nate must've saw me because he took off running back to his car. That was when I decided not to go after him. I put the gun away and scooped Tamir up off the bench. Placing him gently down across the back seat, I jumped back in the car and took off toward the hospital to get Tamir checked out. I attempted to call Major several times while I was on my way there, but he must've been feeling some type of way because his ass wouldn't answer my calls.

Reaching the hospital, I stopped right at the entrance and took Tamir inside. One of Major and San's workers was standing in the front. I tossed him the keys and told him to let Major know I was there with Tamir. I rushed inside and hollered for help. I told the receptionist that Tamir was taken by his father, and since I just found him, he needed to be checked immediately. I knew that was going to spark a fire I probably wasn't ready to face, but I wanted her to check on Tamir and fast. There was no telling what Nate's good-for-nothing ass did to my baby. That wasn't a chance I was willing to take.

By the time Tamir was placed in a room, I could hear a loud ruckus going on around me. I cracked the door to see what was going on, and I saw San and Major coming toward me with a group of niggas I'd never seen before. I hurried to shut the door back and went back over to where Tamir was sitting up playing on the bed. One thing I could say about him was that he was a happy baby. KoKo always protected him from anything bad going on around them. She barely even argued with Nate in front of Tamir. I wasn't sure how she did that, but she always wanted him to see her in a happy way.

"Tamir!" Hassan busted in the room and yelled. He ran toward Tamir, damn near knocking me over.

"Major, can I talk to you?" I asked.

"Naw. You good, ma," he told me. My head turned to the side, and I squinched my eyes up. There was no way he was really that damn mad at me.

"Seriously? We doing this?"

"Yeah, we doing this. You want to be independent, so do it on your own time," he fumed. That shit really bothered me. Why couldn't he understand that I wasn't trying to go against him but that I had to make things right? How many times did he go out the way and do the things he thought was best for him?

"It's not fair, Major. Are you trying to say that we're done?"

"This not about you, Kita. This is about Tamir. We can deal with us later." Hearing him say that really messed me up inside. I'd really started to care for him, and he was about to walk away from me.

"This is about us too. It's about all of us. What kind of shit is this? You are ready to walk away from me when I was trying to do the right thing. How many times have you gone against San? There have been a lot of fuckin' times that you've done it. I've seen him tell you to do shit and you'd do what the fuck you wanted to do on some, 'fuck that nigga' type shit. Now you wanna be a fuckin' hypocrite? What kinda shit is that?" I'd started going off about any and everything that I could think of to make his ass feel bad. He wasn't about to do this shit to me.

"What is she talking about, Major?" San asked. Hearing his voice was the reminder I needed that he was in the room. I snapped my mouth shut before I said anything else that I wasn't supposed to say.

"I don't know what the fuck she talkin' about, and I don't care. She made her choice, and now, I'm makin' mine," he stated and walked around me to go over to Tamir.

"Is everything okay in here?" a nurse popped her head in the room to ask.

"Yeah, stop being nosy, bi—" My statement was interrupted by San.

139

"Everything is fine. Thank you," San told her.

"The doctor should be back in here shortly."

It wasn't long before the doctor came in and told us that Tamir was fine. We all sighed, thankful that Nate didn't take his anger and frustrations with KoKo out on Tamir.

"I'm going to take him up to see KoKo," San announced. "Y'all mufuckas need to figure out what you're going to do because you not about to be acting like this in this hospital. Tamir and KoKo need us right now. Y'all have to deal with what-ever you got going on outside of here," San chided.

"You're right. Don't worry, it won't happen again," Major assured him. They dapped each other up, and San left out of the room.

"Kita, look... I'm not about to do the back-and-forth shit with you. I know that your hood mentality got you thinking everybody out to get you, and that's not the case. I understand that you did what you thought was right, but at the end of the day, the shit was dangerous. You know what I do. The shit ain't no secret. If I tell you to fuckin' do something, I have to trust you enough to know that you're going to do it. I can't work and worry about you at the same fuckin' time because you're so fuckin' hardheaded."

When Major broke shit down to me, I understood what he meant. Before, I thought he was just being him and trying to control me like niggas had done in the past. I didn't want that ever again. What he was telling me was right, and I needed to accept that. There was no way he would be able to go handle his business in the streets if he was constantly worried about what I had going on.

"You're right, and I'm sorry. I promise if you give me one more chance, I won't let this happen again. I'm so used to having to depend on only myself and KoKo that I thought I was doing the right thing. I realize now that I fucked up. Baby, I swear if you give me one more chance, I won't do this shit again."

I'd grown accustomed to being around Major. Everything

about him felt right to me. So why was it so fuckin' hard for me to trust him and know that he wouldn't do anything to hurt me? It was my past experiences with niggas. I'd been hurt before and vowed that I'd never let it happen again. I'd been controlled before and knew that wasn't a situation I could ever see myself being in again.

"I can't do this with you right now." Major came over to me and placed a kiss on my forehead. He tried walking around me, but I dropped down to the floor and grabbed ahold of his leg. Loudly, I began sobbing and praying. Yeah, I was praying that God didn't take this man out of my life. I couldn't care less if someone laughed or talked about me. I knew a good man, and Major was that. "Get up, Kita," he yelled. He was not trying to hide the fact that he was angry with me.

"No. I'm not getting up until you tell me we can work this out."

"Get up, Kita," he repeated. Instead of responding, I shook my head no. "Fuck this shit!" He bent down, put his hands up under my arms and yanked me up off the floor.

Major walked with me until he had me pinned up against the wall. We glared into each other's eyes. I was praying this would make him soften up a bit. That was going to be the only way I'd be able to get him to hear me out.

"I'm sorry. Don't do this."

"I've asked you to stop, and I'm not doing it again. Either you're going to listen to me, or you're going to make this difficult on yourself. You can't fuck up and think I'm just going to let the shit go. I've done it too many times. Now you're going to have to deal with your choices."

Major said what he said and finally placed me back down on my feet. I wrapped my arms around his neck and pulled him in for a kiss. He didn't stop me, so that gave me an ounce of hope. I allowed my tongue to slither inside his mouth. He still didn't stop me. That was when I decided I was going to take things a step further. I moved my hand down to his pants and wrestled with trying to undo his belt so I could get to his hidden treasure. That was when he finally stopped me.

"I'm not about to do this with you. You're not a hoe, so stop acting like one. If you want me to bend you over that bed and fuck the shit out of you, I'll do it. Just know that when I'm done, I'm pulling my pants up and still walking out this bitch like ain't shit happen. Pussy is not what's going to keep me. I don't give a fuck how good it is," he asserted and moved me out the way.

Major walked out the door. He didn't give me a chance to talk to him or say anything else that could potentially make the situation better. The fact that he walked away so easily led me to believe he wasn't fuckin' with me like that in the first place. If he wanted to go, who was I to stop him? His ass just better know that I wasn't about to sit around and decide for him to want to come back.

# ❧ 25 ❧

# MAJOR

It hurt me to the core to have to handle Kita the way that I did. I really wasn't breaking up with her, but like I said, she needed to know that she couldn't keep getting away with doing dumb shit. The shit was just too dangerous.

After I left her in the room, I went down to my car where Domo told me Kita left it. I got the keys from him and got inside. I had to get the fuck away from the hospital. I made sure to text San and let him know what was up.

*Me: I'm out. Take care of your business. I can't deal with shit else tonight.*

*Brother: You good? What happened with your girl?*

*Me: I gotta take a break from her before I go crazy. That damn girl gonna be the death of me... LOL.*

*Brother: I feel ya. Hit one for me too.*

Him telling me to hit one for him too caused me to laugh. I smoked the fuck out of a blunt, but San put that shit down a while ago. He said it fucked with his mental capacity and he needed to be on high alert at all times. I understood that. The shit didn't fuck with me like that, so I had no problems smoking.

It was the wee hours of the morning. The only thing I wanted to do was go home and curl up in my bed. Work was the furthest thing on my mind. I was glad that San got Tamir back and was able to take him to see KoKo. With any luck, that would be what they needed to bring her out of her coma and know that she was going to be fine. She had to be. Tamir needed her. San needed her as well.

My mind was all over the place as I drove, which was all bad. Normally, driving helped me to relax. Not today. I wanted to roll up, but since my head was already fucked up, I figured it would be best for me to do it when I got home. At least then, I wouldn't have to worry about the punk ass police pulling me over and trying to take me to jail.

Finally making it home, I hit my remote to let the garage up. It was too early in the morning to be dealing with bullshit. All I wanted to do was shower and go to sleep. My stomach was growling, but I didn't care. I was too drained to eat.

**Ring... Ring... Ring...**

My phone rang, and I automatically knew who it was. I wasn't changing my number, because I'd had it too long, and I wasn't about to block her, because her lil' crazy ass was going to learn how to listen when I spoke.

"What, Kita?" I answered.

"Why are you doing this to us?" she cried on the other end of the phone.

"I'm not doing anything to us. I want you to listen to me and stop doing all that crying and shit. We gotta take a break. If we don't take it now, there's no way that we'll ever get back together."

"What do you mean by that?"

"I mean that if we stay together and you defy me again, then I'm seriously done with you."

"But I promised you that I wasn't ever going to do that again. I had to do this for myself."

"Listen to you... You had to do this for *yourself*! What about me? What about Tamir? What about KoKo? Shit, we need you too. What if you would've ran your lil' ass out there and Nate really pumped your ass with some hot shit? We would've been fucked up behind that shit, and you would've been gone," I fussed.

"Baby, I know that. I wasn't thinking. I admit that. That's not enough for you to walk away from me. This is our first real problem. You should've told me when you met me that you would leave at the first sign of trouble. How the hell a street nigga running away from a lil' bitty ass woman like me?"

"Street nigga? Mannnn... Fuck outta here with that shit. I'm a whole boss."

"A boss that's running from a chick."

"You ain't no regular chick. You a whole hood chick. Y'all mufuckas crazy. You better talk that shit to someone else," I admitted. Those were facts. Everybody in their right minds knew that when a chick was hood, she was the worst one to cross. Hood chicks were like a whole different breed.

"I'm coming over," she told me.

"No you aren't. Stay wherever the fuck you are. I'm not 'bout to play with you. I'm tired, and I want to get in the bed."

"We both know you get the best sleep when I'm next to you." That was very true. But she'd given me a headache. I wasn't up for dealing with her ass anymore tonight.

"I'm good. You have a good night," I told her and ended the call.

What would be the reason for me to stay on the phone? There wasn't one. She had some growing up to do. If Kita was going to be with me, she had to be on her grown woman shit and let all that hood shit go. It wouldn't be a problem if she knew when and where to turn that shit on and off, but she didn't. She kept that hood mentality from the time she woke up until the time she went to sleep, and that needed to change.

## 26

# HASSAN (SAN)

Tamir lit up the room the moment I walked in. I ran to him, and he threw his little arms around my neck. I swear it felt like I was holding my own child.

Kita and Major stood in the room arguing with each other, and that made me mad because we had other shit to worry about. They should've been happy that Tamir was back safely. Their real concern should've been catching Nate's punk ass and doing what we could to make sure KoKo was good.

Major wasn't the cause of the fighting, but he was just as wrong as Kita was. He allowed her to get away with shit, and she thought it was okay. What did he expect? He should've shut all that shit down the first time she did something he didn't like, then he wouldn't have to worry about her ass doing it again. I learned that shit a long time ago.

"Mommyyyyyy..." Tamir hollered when he laid eyes on KoKo. I got JT to help me dress him in the PPE as I dressed myself in it. I was serious about wanting everybody to be protected when going in the room with her. Nobody was excluded, not even me.

Tamir and I entered the room with KoKo. My heart dropped. I hated seeing her like that. She was always a cheerful and loving woman that everybody loved to be around.

"Tamir, I'm going to sit you up here with your momma. She's not feeling well, so you're going to have to be very careful. Okay?" He nodded his little head.

"What's wong?" he asked. He was trying to say wrong, but since he was so small, I figured he couldn't say it correctly yet. That was fine because I understood exactly what he was trying to say.

"Mommy's sick. She's going to be fine. Talk to her. I'm sure she can hear you." The doctor said that even though she wasn't able to respond, she was able to hear us. That was why I tried to talk to her a lot of the times that I've been around her.

"Mommy, you look funny," Tamir told her and giggled. I couldn't help but laugh too because she did look funny as hell. That made me take my phone out and snap pictures of her alone and then I took pictures of Tamir interacting with her. She was going to love to see this when she came to. I even leaned my big ass down and took a few pictures with her.

The crazy part about all of this was that she looked peaceful. It worried me because it made me start thinking about what my life might be like without her. We hadn't known each other long, but the month that I had known and been around her and Tamir had been the most fulfilling time for me. I didn't want to let that go. I certainly didn't want to imagine my life without Tamir. One thing for damn sure, if KoKo didn't pull out of this shit, there was no way in hell I was letting Nate's ass get anywhere near Tamir.

"Are you ready to go, lil' man?"

"No..." He shook his head. I knew he didn't want to leave KoKo, but he'd been through a lot. I wanted him to get something to eat and get in a bed.

"I'll let you stay a little longer and then we have to go. You need to get your rest. Okay?"

"Okay..." he replied. His lil' baby voice was everything.

While I allowed him to stay to visit with KoKo a little longer, I decided to call Major up and check on him. He could play hard all he wanted, but I knew that he really loved Kita, and holding her accountable for her behavior was really bothering him.

"Sup?" he answered. It was clear that he was tired by the way he sounded on the phone.

"You good, bruh?" I asked him.

"No, but you know how I am. I always bounce back," he truthfully spoke. Major was definitely one of the strongest people I knew. Still, I hated to have to see him hurt behind what was going on with him and Kita. He loved her, whether he wanted to admit it or not.

"You need to talk to her. I know you want to teach her a lesson and that's all good, but you can teach her that lesson while y'all are together. Too much stuff is going on around us right now. You need to keep her protected."

"I'm going to put Domo or JT on her to make sure she good. I just can't be with her right now, because she's either going to get herself killed or me. I'm not ready to die yet. I have so much more I need to do on this earth, and I don't even have a legacy to leave anything to. She gotta get her shit together before I can even pump her up with my seeds."

"Niggaaaaa, I don't care to hear shit about you pumping anybody up with your old ass nut. Hit a blunt and get some sleep. You can think about this shit later today."

"I am. How's Tamir and KoKo?"

"Tamir is in there enjoying his mother's company. I tried to get him to leave to go get something to eat and some sleep, but he doesn't want to leave. I can understand that, but we have to get out of here. I told him I was going to let him visit a little while longer, then we have to go. I'm about to go tell JT that I'm about to go in a few and that I really need him to keep eyes on KoKo. That means you are going to have to put Domo on Kita," I informed him.

"That's cool. Either of them will do. As long as the girls are good, then I'm good."

"A'ight. Bet," I told him.

"What the fuck?" I heard Major say.

"You good, bro? What's going on?" I probed, trying to figure out what the hell was happening.

"How the hell you get in my house?" I heard Major talking, but I never heard anyone responding.

"Major? What the fuck is going on?"

"A'ight. You wanna break into my shit? I got you. Stand right the—"

***Pow...***

Major's words were cut off by a gunshot.

"Major? Bro? What the fuck?" I kept yelling into the phone, but the line went dead.

Tamir was playing with KoKo's hands and singing some little song to her. Not wanting to disturb him, I used that as my chance to go find JT. I tried to remain as calm as possible to not alert any of the medical staff that something was wrong. That didn't stop me from damn near jogging to where I last saw JT.

My phone was still in my hand. I kept dialing Major's number hoping he would pick up and let me know that he was good. I took my eyes off my phone for a second and glanced up. My phone instantly dropped to the ground along with my bottom lip as I peeked up for a brief moment and saw JT and Kita standing in the hallway kissing.

(TO BE CONTINUED...)

CPSIA information can be obtained
at www.ICGtesting.com
Printed in the USA
LVHW091757030921
696898LV00002B/73